Play To Kiss

The Twisted Trilogy: 1
By ARIZONA TAPE

D1518405

Copyright

Trigger warning

This book is a twisted lesfic romance, with a lot of sensitive and harsh topics. Be mindful when you read. Please read with caution.

Prologue

THE FAMILIAR RUSH OF adrenaline danced through my veins as I breathed in the heartbreak on my last victim's face. She'd been far too easy to seduce, but still, the devastation in her eyes excited me. For a moment, I dropped my carefully sculpted mask and flashed her a smile. My real smile.

Her heart broke all over again as I shattered her beautiful illusion of me. She would never trust again. Oh, how it enthralled me. Their pain was addicting and I just couldn't get enough. But who to play with next?

My eyes fell on an image in the newspaper and a wicked grin tugged on the corners of my mouth. A princess? Now that sounded like a fun challenge. After all, the housewives and college girls were boring me. I needed something new, something... *Exciting.*

Gently, I stroked the image of princess Zafira and wished it was her soft cheek I was touching instead.

Soon. Yes, very soon.

Nobody, not even royalty, could escape the twisted games I liked to play.

Chapter 1. Zafira

KILL ME NOW. Well, that wasn't a very proper thought, not for a princess at least. But then again, was there an accurate way to describe the mind-numbing sensation ceremonies brought along? *Throw me off the balcony?*

Whichever way it was, as long as it got me out of this ceremony. I didn't have the slightest interest in whatever rich and spoilt princess Father invited as my brother's future wife. Why they kept insisting I attended these gatherings was a mystery. I had nothing to say, and even if I had, I wasn't allowed to speak anyway. Not in front of the men. I was just to be seated, nice and quiet, next to Mother. Boring, if you asked me.

At least I had a good place to inspect the men and women tending to my family. Some old farts, a handful of young girls who I had no doubt we acquired through slavery, and endless women that thought they would get a better life if they served the royal family. They probably did. Living in the beautiful palace was presumably a lot better than their tents and clay houses. At least, I figured it was. I hadn't actually ever been inside one the houses of the plebs. Now, *that* wouldn't be very proper.

I never set foot outside of the royal grounds, not that I remembered anyway. It was bothersome, but not the worst bit of my existence. The worst part was Oumar, my annoying older brother. The jewel of the family and heir to the throne.

A big mistake, if I did say so myself. The only reason he was the next-in-line was his place in the order we were born. And unfortunately, he had two years on me. At least I seemed to have inherited all the brains of the family. All he had going for him were his good looks, or so I heard the servants whisper. But then again, I couldn't complain. Mother was rumoured to be the most beautiful woman in the whole of our country. That was why Father acquired her. Not a particularly bad thing. As it happened, I was a spitting image of her. But I could only spend that much time looking in the mirror. After a while, even my own reflection became boring.

Just like these ceremonies.

I wondered which prissy would make a big entrance and try to please my unpleasable brother. He was spoilt, through and through. Courtesy of my parents, of course.

The heavy doors were swung open by the palace guards and in came a rather small company. That was surprising. No parade, no fireworks, no naked belly-dancers or carriage with endless gifts? That was new.

I bent slowly to the left and whispered to my handmaiden. "Jamila, who are we welcoming today?"

"The entourage of His Serene Highness Franz and Princess Jade, from a small country in the West, Your Royal Highness, Zafira."

I nodded and dismissed her with a small wave of my fan. I studied the slender woman approaching us and the two men by her side. That was a very small concession. How unusual. Where did they leave the rest of their servants?

The three guests halted in front of the throne and bowed respectfully. The herald on Father's left side cleared his throat and also bowed to us.

"Your Majesty, Your Royal Highness, the honour is mine to present to you the royal entourage from Liechtenstein. His Serene Highness Franz, accompanied by Princess Jade, who come bearing gifts of good will towards you."

He received a short nod from Father and bowed even deeper than before. Urgh, all the bowing was fun in the beginning, but after years and millions of bows, it became tedious. The respect was great and all, but what a waste of time.

And this girl, this princess, looked just as boring as all of them. What she lacked in personality, she probably made up for with money. In a moment, she would bow to my brother and kiss his feet. Figuratively, hopefully. Literally, if she really wanted to be approved by Father.

What was her name again? Jade? Pretty. And boring. Royals just couldn't stop flaunting their status. At least she wasn't called Diamond or Vulcan Rock. Now *that* would be weird, but interesting.

She smiled politely and batted her eyelashes at Oumar. My brother perked up a little and I couldn't blame him. As much as I hated to admit it, Jade was a natural beauty, there was no denying that. But we had many gorgeous princesses asking for his hand and he refused all of them. Not even the most radiant beauty would catch his attention, but this woman seemed to peak his interest? I needed to keep that in mind.

Involuntarily, I snuck another glance at Jade and caught something bizarre. I wasn't sure if I saw it right, but then again... An eye roll wasn't easily mistaken for something else. Unless she had something in her eye?

"Your Majesty, Your Royal Highness, I'm honoured to be in your presence," she smiled, but as soon as she did, I noticed another very brief flicker in her eyes. She was definitely hiding some sarcasm under there.

Huh.

I perked up as I studied the beautiful woman in front of me. A princess with some backbone? Now that could be fun. It had been a good while since we had new people in the palace to play with. Maybe she could entertain me for a bit until I left her for dead in the desert. That sounded like an entertaining idea. Or I could use her to distract my brother...

I motioned Jamila and tilted my fan a little so I didn't disturb anyone. "Where are they staying?"

"In the Summer Resort, Your Royal Highness."

Good, nice and close by. "For how long?"

"The Sultan has invited them to stay for as long as Prince Oumar sees fit. He is very optimistic about this arrangement."

"Thank you." I brushed her away and glanced over my fan at Jade. My brother could spend his whole life believing he was in control, but I knew better. She'd be my plaything long before he even touched her with one finger.

Yes, I deserved some fun. And she would be my new target. After all, I could only toy with so many people inside the palace until Father caught wind of my... nature.

Chapter 2. Mint

OUMAR BECKONED ONE of his servants to come and whispered something. Quickly, the young man ran to Father and relayed the message. From the satisfied smile on Father's face, I could tell Oumar was interested in this... Jade.

Good.

Father clapped his hands and as if shaken awake, the whole throne room came to life. Even at his old age, he commanded a great deal of respect and one would never have guessed he was terminally ill.

The melodic music of our royal orchestra broke the tense silence and the scent of mint and chilli mingled between us. A feast for the plebs. A regular meal for us. Daintily, I nibbled on a piece of freshly baked naan and let the spices dance on my palate. I wasn't allowed to eat a lot as not to lose my figure, but that was fine by me. I enjoyed my slender build, it made people underestimate me.

I waved Jamila over and she brought the handkerchief with mint essence I always dabbed on my wrists. When we were children, my best friend used to joke it covered up the stench of my bad soul when I showed her just a little too much of my personality. From the pained eyes she had when I had her flogged, I knew that regret about the joke was the last thing she felt before her world turned dark.

"I'm going for a walk in the palace gardens and I would very much love if Princess Jade would accompany me," I whispered in her ear. It sounded like an invitation, but we both knew it was an order. As long as Father or Oumar didn't speak, my word was law. And the servants knew better than to disobey me.

Jamila bowed and without ever turning her back to me, shuffled away from my seat. Of all the people in this palace, she was almost tolerable. Quiet and obedient, she never questioned any of my orders and seemed to be as invisible as a slave could be. Yes, she did her job well and it pleased me to have her as my lackey. I should send gifts of gratitude to her family, just so she wouldn't forget the benefits of serving me well. So far, the grain had bought her complete loyalty, but if it ever wavered, I'd have no trouble sending threats.

With a flick of my wrist, I gave the palace master permission to approach the royal seating area.

"What can I do for you, Your Royal Highness Zafira?" he asked submissively, bowing so far down that his nose touched the ground. Urgh, I thoroughly disliked him. He was a massive bootlicker and idolised Father to the point of idiocy. There was nothing about Father that deserved any idolising.

"Send two units of grain to my handmaiden's family right away."

He wavered slightly. "But His Majesty has a strict regimen in place that doesn't allow any goods to be moved without his permission."

Anger bubbled up in my gut as he voiced his defiance. He was in no position to question my orders and I would make damn sure he knew it. "When Jamila's family starves to death, you can personally hand-deliver the news to her. I'm sure she will thank you for not bending the rules for her, just like you will be thankful when your family no longer receives *any* of their benefits."

He turned pale under my unspoken threat and bowed once more. With trembling hands he backed away, not daring to look me in the eye anymore. "Forgive me, it will be done, as you wish, Your Royal Highness."

Without wasting another word on him, I dismissed his presence, confident he would follow my orders. I drew a fake smile on my face and turned around. "Father, the weather is absolutely delightful. Would you please excuse me as I visit our beautiful gardens?" I asked, pretending to be the doting daughter he believed I was. Mother shot me a disapproving glare for not using Father's proper title in public, but I ignored her as always. Calling him Father tugged on his heartstrings and being allowed to call him Father in front of everyone else showed my position in the hierarchy.

He gave me one of his rare smiles and nodded, his permission undisputable even for Mother. She just couldn't stand he favoured me over her.

Triumphantly, I removed myself from the banquet and my maids scurried around to grab refreshments and the palanquin. "I'll walk," I said, not wanting my conversations with the princess to be overheard. It was a mistake to treat the servants as if they were invisible and speaking freely around them was dangerous. We had a lot of enemies that would spend a fortune to get the inside scoop of our palace. It was rather annoying that this policy forbade any kind of social media, but our privacy was far too valuable. It also made life rather tedious. But not for much longer. I just had this feeling that Jade would bring me some well-needed entertainment, whether she wanted to or not.

The gardens were decorated with beds of colourful flowers and they had the scent to match. I pressed my handkerchief against my nose as not to breathe in the pollen and get suffocated by the thick odour they spread. I didn't particularly like the garden, but it was the only place I could talk without being eavesdropped on. Waiting in the shade of the argania trees, I watched Princess Jade being escorted outside and ushered to me.

She intrigued me. Why hadn't she brought a concession along? Something was fishy about her and I wanted to find out.

"Your Royal Highness, Princess Jade is delighted to accept your invitation to the gardens," Jamila introduced her, bowing as she left us to it. She quickly gathered any servants in the vicinity and I knew she was ordering them to leave us. Yes, she was a good handmaiden. I did love being in a position of power, but even if I hadn't been born in it, I would've made it happen. I had a gift for getting my way.

Chapter 3. Innocent

"YOUR ROYAL HIGHNESS, you wanted to see me?" Jade said, bending the knee slightly as she presented herself to me.

"Princess Jade, thank you for gracing me with your presence," I replied, playing by all the rules of etiquette. I was going to be so polite, she'd never suspect anything. Oh, the fun it would be.

"It's entirely my pleasure," Jade said, her voice sweet as honey. That was very submissive of her and I wondered where the sarcastic part had gone. The feisty part that dared roll her eyes during such an important ceremony.

"Walk with me," I commanded, making sure to match my tone to hers. She wasn't the only one who could play the innocent girl. "Stay," I barked at Jamila, making sure that none of my handmaidens actually followed us into the lush garden. The blonde princess hurried behind me, matching my pace perfectly while staying just one step behind me. Good girl, she had been taught well.

"You certainly command a great deal of respect," Jade noted, the admiration shining through in her words.

"You flatter me, Princess Jade," I said, hiding any emotion from my voice. I didn't need it, if she was smart, she'd catch my implications.

"I apologise, you don't need my flattery, Your Highness," she added quickly, almost remorseful.

"You're right, I don't," I said abruptly. I turned in my step and stared intensely into her eyes. They were as green as the brightest gem and her name didn't do their beauty justice. She was undeniably stunning and that pleased me. A woman like her would certainly not be familiar with being the second most beautiful woman in the room. Her perfect green eyes had nothing against my almond shaped ones. My fair appearance would make her uncomfortable, even if she never realised why.

"My deepest apologies, I didn't mean to insult you in any way," she spoke, bowing slightly in regret.

"What brings you here, Princess?" I asked with a directness nobody would expect from the timid princess they all thought I was. Maybe my bluntness would spook her and her mask would slip just enough for me to see what was behind it.

"I've traveled here to see your brother, Crown Prince Oumar, and arrange an alliance through marriage. Did my servants misinform the palace about my visit?" she replied, frowning her perfectly shaped eyebrows in confusion.

I paused and glared deep into her eyes. "And you really want to marry my brother?"

"With all my heart, Your Highness," she answered, staring at me with such a convincing look I would've believed her if it hadn't been for the eyeroll I caught earlier.

"Tell me, what do you desire most about him?"

"I..." Jade hesitated, as if she wasn't sure how open she could be. She didn't need to, I had enough examples.

"His riches, his palace, his name?" I summed up, far blunter than I should've been. But something about her rubbed me the wrong way. She was far too innocent for that eye roll to be an accident. And I wanted to know what it was about.

"You insult me, Your Highness," she protested, her voice cracking slightly as she defended her honour. If she even had any. My brother was one of the most detestable people I had the displeasure of knowing, nobody came here to marry him for him. They were all after the spoils and power a marriage would bring, but I would never let that happen. There was no way that Oumar would actually inherit the throne, not while I breathed. I just needed to find the right moment to erase his existence and take his place as the heir I was meant to be. Although maybe... I'd seen the glint in Oumar's eyes as he watched her. Maybe I could use her to finally get rid of my spoilt brother once and for all. Yes, that was a good idea. But for that, I needed to make her trust me. I needed to make her believe I had her best interests at heart. And that started with changing the tension hanging between us.

"I apologise, Princess Jade. I believe the afternoon sun is affecting my mood. Pardon me for my outspoken words."

"There is nothing to forgive, Your Highness," she smiled, waving away my gracious gesture.

"Please, I'd love to make your acquaintance."

"It's as if it never happened, Your Highness." Jade bowed and a whiff of her perfume caught my nose. Vanilla. My favourite.

"Wouldn't you agree that in the company we keep, those titles become more of an annoyance than gestures of respect?" I said, deciding that making her feel like she was on equal footing with me would help with earning her trust. I just needed to get close enough so I could find out what made her tick and how she thought. Long enough until I knew how to play her like a fiddle and make the most beautiful music. A melody of destruction and disaster, and nobody would ever know I was the maestro behind the ballad of despair.

"Your Royal Highness?" Jade asked, tilting her head ever so slightly.

"Please do call me Zafira," I said, gracing her with a privilege that not many had experienced.

"Your Highness, you honour me," she gasped, clasping her hands in front of her mouth as she bowed deeply.

"If you are to be wedded to my brother, I want to welcome to you with open arms," I lied, hoping she would believe that was what I actually wanted.

"I'm truly overjoyed," she spoke. She sounded genuinely surprised and grateful and I wondered if perhaps I mistook the eye roll for something it wasn't. Maybe she had a little fleck of dust in her eye and she was really this daft and sweet?

That would be a lot duller, but I didn't care. It was time to kick my brother dear off his throne and claim the kingdom for myself, before Father kicked the bucket. And if I needed to use this dumb goose, I would. And I'd make sure to play with her until she thoroughly regretted the moment she decided to set foot in my palace.

I extended my hand as a test, wondering if she'd kiss it or shake it. Whichever she did, would reveal something about her she might not want to show.

"I'm Zafira, it's a true pleasure to meet you," I introduced myself informally, something my esteemed parents wouldn't have approved off. None of my royal ancestors would have.

And that made it even more exciting. Every rule was meant to be broken.

"Jade. And the pleasure is all mine, Your Hi— I mean, Zafira." Jade pressed her hand in mine as she stared deep into my eyes. Green to brown. A spark jumped from her skin onto mine. A spark that could've easily been mistaken for static electricity, but I knew better. This was something entirely else.

I hadn't been mistaken, she was not the shy and sweet girl she pretended to be. She hadn't even flinched when she shook my hand. No, she was far too gutsy to be the ditzy princess she made herself out to be. And I couldn't wait to discover all her desires and weaknesses.

"I will retreat to my quarters now, but I look forward to our next meeting." I dipped my head, dismissing her kindly but firmly.

"As do I. Your kindness and hospitality have made me feel most welcome," Jade replied, bowing as she shuffled backwards. The moment she put a couple of metres between us, my handmaidens rushed towards me with their canopy and refreshments. Annoyed, I waved them away. As much as I enjoyed being tended to, they were overbearing and treated me like a helpless little girl. And it was time to show the world what I was capable of.

Without taking my eyes off of the blonde and her swaying hips, I watched her exit the gardens. There was no doubt that she was rejoining her small party again and would tell them all about my generosity and kindness. Yes, this was a great start to the beginning of Oumar's end.

Surprised, I noted my elevated heartbeat as I stared at Jade. I was more excited than I expected to be, than I had been in a long time. How uncommon. How perfect.

Time to play.

Chapter 4. Summer Resort

"JAMILA, I WANT TO KNOW everything there is to know about Princess Jade," I ordered, beckoning my handmaiden to come closer. She quickly rushed to my side, kneeling next to my seat.

"Your Highness?"

"They must have brought servants with them. I want you to figure out as much as you can about Jade. I want to know about every step she takes in this palace, about every word she whispers, about every breath of air she takes."

"Of course, as you wish," she said compliantly, but I heard the unspoken question in her tone. Jamila was never good at hiding her emotions and that was one of the reasons why she was perfect for me. I could read her like an open book.

"If she is about to marry our beloved Crown Prince, it's our duty to make sure she deserves his company," I lied, spinning a tale she'd take to heart. I found people were most easily manipulated if they genuinely believed in what they were doing, even if that wasn't what I was after. But that wasn't really my problem.

Jamila's eyes lit up and she nodded obediently. "You're so clever, my princess. I will investigate as thoroughly as possible."

"Perfect. Just make sure to keep this between us. We wouldn't want her to catch wind of our little secret," I smiled, playing my handmaiden like I always had. She admired me like a big sister and I knew just how to make her feel included enough in my life that she obeyed me like a lap dog. She was far too easy to play, but it was convenient. Especially when I was expanding and needed more intel about my next target. I'd turn Jade into my next pawn. The last pawn I needed that would finally get me the throne.

"That'll do for today, please take your leave," I ordered, dismissing Jamila from my quarters. The night was falling and it was finally time to play.

The benefits of not having to sleep a lot were definitely paying off. It gave me a couple of hours of breathing room where the guards and servants weren't watching my every move. I clicked a secret compartment open underneath my bed and revealed a heavy cloak. The dark patterns blended perfectly with the shadows dancing through the palace at night. Like a snake, I slithered through the halls, unseen and unheard. The flowers in the garden were all closed, but the thick scent still hung in the air. The grass ritsled as I brushed through it and hurried away from the walls and into the night. I pressed my cloak against my mouth as not to breathe in any impurities in the heavy air and give away my position by sneezing. The changing of the guards gave me the perfect window to sneak out and visit the Summer Resort. This was their first night in a foreign environment and they hadn't had time to adapt or change themselves yet. And I wanted an untainted picture of them.

A lone bird screeched in the fields and I held my breath, freezing against the rough bark of a tree. Cautiously, I scanned the horizons for any movement or sounds.

One... Two... Three... Four... Five... I counted, not daring to move until I was absolutely sure there were no unplanned eyes on the garden.

Six... Seven... Eight... Nine... Ten... Everything stayed quiet and I counted on the short attention span of the guards not to keep looking for whatever snuck through the night. With an elevated heartbeat, I weaved through the shadows until I reached the secret entry to the Summer Resort. The rusty door shrieked softly as I entered the residence and snuck through the maze of stairs up to one of the hidden balconies. From this place, I'd have a perfect view of the courtyard and hopefully, get a good listen of the private conversations our guests had. Nothing that happened between our palace walls would stay a secret to me. I settled myself on one of the stone arches and waited patiently for the cool air to tempt the guests outside.

"Beautiful, wouldn't you agree?"

Startled, I jumped up and stared at the back of the room. My gaze was met by the most brilliant pair of smouldering green eyes and a thrill of electricity traveled down my spine.

Busted.

For the first time, someone caught me spying on them. And I wasn't sure if I should be livid or impressed.

"What is?" I asked, wondering if she just gave me a compliment.

She prepped her shoulder against the wall and pointed up to the sky. "The stars."

I nodded, brushing off her earlier vagueness. "Absolutely breathtaking," I agreed, but I wasn't talking about the heavenly bodies. Or at least, not the one I was looking at right now.

"I wish I'd have known you would grace us with a visit, Zafira. I'd have prepared instead of welcoming you on this cold balcony," she smiled and for the life of me, I couldn't work out if she meant it or if it was a nudge to my uninvited entry.

"This balcony suits me just fine," I replied, crossing my arms defensively. She seemed... Different than before. Less innocent... Less.... Hmmm...

"In what way can I assist you, Princess Zafira?" she asked, but unlike any of my servants, it didn't sound very submissive. Instead there was a hint of something else, something dangerous. Something I wanted to play with.

"What makes you believe you can assist me, Jade?" I answered boldly, letting the pleasantries be for what they were. Every royal knew they were just for appearance sake and right now, there was nobody to listen to our untainted words.

"Well, what else could've brought you here?" she smiled, her green eyes shimmering in the starlight.

I lifted my eyebrow. "So your natural assumption is that I'm here for you?" I asked, challenging her. The shy and timid woman I saw earlier seemed to have completely gone, and yet, I couldn't exactly figure out who I had standing in front of me.

"Aren't you?" she shot back, meeting my gaze with the same intensity. For a moment, I just stared at her, wondering if she'd take her words back. This was my world, this was my palace, and she was definitely walking on thin ice. But that didn't seem to deter her, in fact, it only seemed to spur her on.

Her confidence was annoying me a little, and yet, denying it seemed like showing weakness. "Yes, I am," I confessed, hoping that my boldness would shock her as much as hers had surprised me.

"What an honour." Jade pushed herself away from the wall. Her heels clacked on the marble floor as they echoed softly into the night. A whiff of a scent I couldn't identify curled in my nose and it annoyed me more than I wanted to admit that I didn't know what it was. Lilies? Honeysuckle? It was something floral, but it wasn't light and sweet like the mask she wore when she entered our palace. It was heavy and seductive, like a carnivorous plant attracting bees only to trap them in their petals forever. She was alluring and tempting, bewitching and enchanting, in a way that I hadn't experienced in a woman before. It felt dark, exhilarating, dangerous. She'd be a challenge to break, but once I did, it would be so worth it. Oh, I couldn't wait to turn this prideful woman into my puppet and use her for my own gains.

Yes, this was the opportunity I'd been waiting for. The thrill I was looking for and I couldn't love it more.

Chapter 5. Prince

"ISN'T SHE BEAUTIFUL, sister?" Oumar said as he pointed to the foreigners strolling through the garden. Jade was whispering to her brother in what looked like a very intimate conversation as they admired the exquisite gardens we kept.

Interesting... I could use Franz as a way to get leverage on his sister and I knew exactly how.

"Zaf?" Oumar nudged me and pointed towards the blonde drawing all eyes to her.

"She is perfect, my dearest brother," I replied, drawing one of my fake smiles to the surface. He didn't have the slightest idea of the twisted thoughts I had in my head, of my motives to steal the throne. In his eyes, I was his sweet sister that supported him in all his endeavours. When I struck, he wouldn't know what hit him.

"Jamila," I called, waving impatiently at the group of maids tending to me.

"Yes, Your Highness?" She scurried to my side, the fan wafting some cool air in my face.

"I will take a stroll in the garden and join His Serene Highness' company," I announced, getting up without waiting for her reply. All of my servants were trained to shadow me perfectly and if I had to wait for them, they'd be out of here before they could blink an eye. I didn't need to adjust to them, they needed to match me.

The sun strained into my skin and I glared behind me, wondering who was responsible for the canopy and why she was lagging behind.

"I'm burning," I scoffed, mentally picking out who to punish. Jamila clapped her hands, snapping the shade slave out of her trance and she hurried to my side.

"Your Highness, please forgive her. Aliyah is new in her service, she meant no harm," my handmaiden apologised, falling to my feet. I pulled up my nose, the wrath inside of me swirling like a roaring dragon. How dared she hire someone new without my consent?

"You *dare* hire new help that isn't properly trained?" I hissed, containing my temper since I was on public display. I didn't need anyone catching on to the rage inside of me.

"Forgive me, I meant no harm, I just didn't want to burden you with my incompetence," Jamila cried, kissing the hem of my dress in shame.

"I'll deal with you later," I snapped, yanking the delicate fabric out of her hands. I didn't need salt stains on it. I pointed at Farah, the second in rank, and snapped my fingers impatiently. Greedy to step up and get in my good graces, she quickly barked at the maids and had them scrambling around me in half a second.

With my nose in the air, I left Jamila sobbing in the dust, unworthy of my attention. I'd punish her later for this indecency and her regret would haunt her for the rest of her life. Just how I liked it.

I pushed any anger to the back and drew a fake smile to my lips. With all the innocence in the world, I approached Franz and from the light in his eyes, I knew I immediately had his full attention. Perfect.

Respectfully, I bowed slightly at the royal pair, catching Jade's gaze as I did. She seemed as modest and sweet as the first time, but I knew I saw a different side of her last night. A true side of her. I just needed to figure out this woman with the almost-perfect mask.

To gauge her reaction, I turned completely to Franz, deciding to ignore her for now. I wanted to see just how interested she was.

"My dear Prince, are you enjoying the wonderful gardens?" I asked politely, engaging in the small talk we royals were so well-versed in.

"The gardens are almost the most beautiful thing in here," he said, turning towards me. "Almost," he emphasised, the sun reflecting in his sapphire eyes. They were almost as striking as his sister's. *Almost*.

"Have you seen our fountains?" I added, turning my back to Jade as I fleetingly touched his arm. He caught my gesture and something flashed across his face. Something I couldn't recognise just yet. But I would figure it out. I would figure out everything there was to know about him and use it against him and everyone he loved. Even Jade. I quickly glanced at the blonde. Especially Jade.

"They were built as an ode to my mother," I narrated, guiding the prince through the maze of fountains. I knew Jade was trotting along, just one beat behind me. I hoped me ignoring her was annoying her. It just had to be.

"It's stunning. Everything here is absolutely exquisite," he smiled, clearly using his big-boy words. Briefly, I let my hand linger on his arm as I steered him towards the secluded part. The daylight shone through the collection of gems and cast colourful patterns on the ground. With the glimmer of the dancing water and the glint of the jewels, there was an indescribable beauty in front of me. And yet, I only had eyes for Jade.

Chapter 6. Aliyah

I LEFT FRANZ ADMIRING the artwork to steal a glance at the blonde with the green eyes. For a split second, the ditzy grin fell from her face and she flashed me a seductive smile.

There, right there. I knew there was something else going on behind the innocent facade and I was dying to find out. But how was I going to draw out that side of her? How would I lure out the predator? By confronting her? Tricking her? Setting a trap?

Yes, that would work... A metaphorical trap with bait she wouldn't be able to resist, that no one ever had been able to.

Me.

I'd be the prey that she'd chase, right up until the moment that I'd turn around and reveal my teeth. Right before she couldn't turn around. Right before it'd be too late.

I had been playing the sweet girl for my whole life, it would be a piece of cake to convince Jade I was easy prey. I just needed to give her the opportunity to get close to me. But how?

"Princess, I've heard about the wonders of the exotic animals roaming around in the forests. Are the legends true?" Franz asked.

I dipped my head. "The beasts are as wild as one could imagine, with fierce eyes and thunderous roars," I said, even though I had no clue of knowing.

"That sounds absolutely stunning. While we stay here and our siblings get acquainted, perhaps we should too?" he proposed cheekily. If it had been anyone else, I'd have had him flogged by the end of the day. But not now, not when I saw an opening.

"I'd be honoured to accompany you," I lied, a plan brewing in my head.

"It shall be my honour," Franz complimented, bending down to kiss the back of my hand. I swallowed my disgust as he smacked his wet lips on my skin and instead, smiled politely like I did best. I waved at my servants and bowed every so slightly towards our guests.

"Your Serene Highness," I smiled, lingering just a second too long. I had no doubt Jade would've noticed. From the glint in her eyes as I turned to her, I knew I was right. "Princess."

She returned my greeting with a polished smile of her own. A darkness flicked through her eyes and the angered glint satisfied me more than I expected. With the excitement building in my stomach, I turned away. Farah snapped her fingers and my servants jumped to life. Time to find out what she was made off.

"Have Jamila and the new girl escorted to the dungeons. And make sure Halim is present."

"Of course, Your Highness." She turned to bark orders to the other maids, but I caught her before she did.

"Personally," I scolded, shaking my head in disappointment. I didn't need a handmaiden that was afraid to get her own hands dirty. If I made a request, I needed her to know when it was personal or a task for the others. She still had a lot to learn.

With my nose in the air, I left the guests and made my way to the dungeon. Time for Jamila's punishment. Oh, she was going to regret this mistake. I would make sure of it.

The damp air of the cellars clashed against my throat and I gagged slightly. I hated coming down here, but it couldn't be helped. She needed to learn her place and that was just a fact.

"Your Royal Highness," Jamila cried, falling to her knees in front of me. Tears drew silver lines on her cheeks like paint on a canvas. The other girl, I'd already forgotten her name, mimicked my handmaiden yet she didn't seem as distraught. She truly was new. She had no idea what I was capable of. Yet.

I turned to Farah, inspecting her from top to toe. She looked just a little too gleeful for my taste and I'd have to make it very clear that she wasn't my new favourite.

"Leave," I barked. Her face fell and she opened her mouth in what I assumed would be a protest. "Not one word."

Promptly, she bowed and scuffled away. Bad luck for her today. With her out of the way, I focused back on the two women in front of me.

"Halim, whip," I commanded, pointing at the rack of weapons hidden in one of the crevices of the dungeon. This was my personal playground. Nobody ever came here besides me and Halim, the youngest son of the palace master. He had a dark streak in him that I appreciated and only discovered accidentally. The pleasures of having eyes everywhere. After I found out, I turned him into my personal torturer, leaving him to do the dirty work.

"Jamila, how many lashes do you deserve today?" I asked her, the power dancing through my veins. She shot me a pained look, no doubt remembering the agreement we had between us. I always let her pick the amount of whippings, but if she chose too little, I'd double them.

"At least twenty, Your Highness," she whimpered, her whole body tensing as she groveled in front of me.

"How many lashes does she deserve?" I added, circling the other woman. Amiya? Alicia? Aliyah? That sounded right. Aliyah.

"Please, Your Highness. It was all my fault, she doesn't deserve—"

"Are you to decide what she deserves?" I snapped, cutting her off. Jamila quickly shook her head, trembling under my command.

"I apologise, please, I beg you."

"You beg for what?" I grinned, allowing some of my real nature to show. Still, I couldn't completely let myself go. The only way I'd ever show my real nature was if I was sure the person I showed it to could never speak again. And I didn't feel like silencing all three of them. That was just a little too excessive. *For now.*

"Please, don't hurt the girl. It's all my fault, I take full blame. Please, just punish me," she mewled, her hands shaking as she crawled to my feet. "I beg you, Your Highness, have mercy—"

"Mercy?" I lashed out, kicking her away. "Are you saying I'm not merciful?"

"No, no, not at all. I misspoke, please, I beg you, I—"

"Halim. The whip." I held out my hand and the young man handed me the crop. The leather shrieked in my hand, tight and smooth. The material would draw streams of pain across her back, she'd feel the open wounds with every turn she'd make in bed at night or every movement during the day. And yet, they were perfectly hideable. Nobody would ever know what artwork I painted on her back. The perfect weapon.

Threateningly, I stretched the lashes between my hands, curling them around my arm before I cracked them into the silence. The two women flinched in fear and satisfaction curled through me. There was something pure, something beautiful about the panic in their eyes. It was... honest. Consuming. It showed true emotion, an emotion I almost understood.

Jamila shut her eyes, preparing for the stinging pain on her back and for a moment, I waited, basking in the tension of her fear. Beautiful.

Twang.

Chapter 7. Whip

WITH A SNAP, I THREW the whip down in front of her. Surprised, Jamila's eyes flew open and she stared questioningly at me. I grinned, not explaining myself. It was all the more fun to watch someone connect the dots I drew. She inspected the whip for another moment. The pathetic tears on her face dried and the fear in her eyes turned to dark horror.

"No..." she gasped, her hands flying to her mouth, but it was no use. A loud sob escaped her lips and she fell to the floor once again. "Please, Your Highness, please don't make me do this... Please, I can't... I can't."

I stepped back, hiding my smile in the darkness of the dungeons. "Either you draw ten lines on her back with this whip or Halim will punish her with twenty lashes. Your choice."

"Princess, please... I can't, I can't do this. Not me," she whimpered pathetically, crawling over the rough floor as the sniveling coward she was.

I crouched down next to her, my voice softer than it had been the whole time. "Listen, Jamila. You have a choice here to save your friend a whole lot of pain. It's up to you to how much she suffers. That is your reward for serving me so well. The twenty lashes you receive afterwards will be your punishment," I said calmly, trapping her in one of my twisted webs. There was no reward, no on the contrary, the whole of this was her punishment. Whether she watched Aliyah being whipped to a devastating state or she inflicted the pain herself, this would haunt her for life. She would feel guilty about this until her last breath. I would make sure of it.

"Princess—"

"Your choice, Jamila. Choose wisely. Ten or twenty. What shall it be?"

"Please," she begged, her tears drawing new rivers of pain across her cheeks.

"Ten or twenty."

The wails of the griping woman stopped and for a moment, a heavy silence hung in the dark dungeon. Halim drew in a sharp breath and I knew this was exciting him. I could imagine his hardened cock strained against his pants from the power display. He loved weakness portrayed on hopeless faces and his dark desires made him the perfect tool. He'd never be able to expose me without revealing his own twisted nature. For now, I allowed him to live out his fantasies by using him to fulfil my own.

"Ten," Jamila whispered, her pain echoing through the dungeon. Excitement curled around me and I silenced the thrill shooting through my veins. There was an innocence and sweetness to Jamila, a purity that I was about to taint forever. Having her whip this young woman would carve invisible scars into her soul forever, lines that she could never rid herself off. How exhilarating.

"Halim, bind her," I ordered, pointing at the youngest of the two. The crude man rearranged his trousers and with a devious grin, he yanked Aliyah to the wooden contraption. She sobbed quietly as the rough ropes dug into her skin, chaining her without the possibility of escape. With tear-stained eyes, she stared up at me and wept, and yet, she didn't even protest. Pathetic.

"I'm waiting, Jamila," I sang, taking seat on one of the ridges. The air was thick with anticipation and I felt it tighten my stomach. I was ready.

The leather shrieked as my handmaiden coiled her hand around the handle, drawing the long whip back in hesitation. Tremors took a hold of her body and fear made itself home in her eyes.

"Please," she tried again, begging me for something she'd never get. She deserved to be punished, they both did.

"One more word and I'll make it fifteen," I threatened, glaring at her sternly. I needed her to understand this wasn't optional, I needed her to draw permanent lines in Aliyah's back. After tonight, Jamila would never do anything without my permission and that was just how I liked my servants. Total obedience.

My handmaiden dried her cheeks, balling her fists in determination. The air crackled with anticipation and I held my breath, not wanting to break the moment.

The whip cracked and the dungeon filled itself with one haunting scream. Jamila hadn't used full force and I knew this wasn't the most painful strike. But I knew this one was the one that would stay with her the longest. This stroke didn't just tear her blouse and skin open, it tore the trust she had in Jamila apart. Their relationship was forever ruined, gone like dust in the wind. Now they were just my pawns and I could play them any way I wanted.

Together with the cracks of the whip, Aliyah's wails echoed against the walls, the terror in her voice colouring the air with trauma. She'd be haunted, forever haunted by the thunder of a whip. And Jamila? Jamila would never disappoint me ever again.

Reduced to a sobbing mess, the slender woman trembled in her bounds. Blood trickled down her back, mingling with the dust on the floor and Jamila's tears of devastation. I exchanged a glance with Halim and caught the lust in his eyes. There was no doubt about how excited he had gotten and I would make sure he'd live out all his twisted fantasies.

"Can I humbly request to flog the second one, Your Highness?" he asked, his voice shaking eagerly. I held a scoff back, not wanting to show my disgust in him. He was animalistic, feeding off of his primal desires. No restraint, no brains, no mind. He was just another one of my tools, a weapon that I wielded to terrify my victims.

The whip fell out of Jamila's exhausted hands and she fell to the floor. The splattered blood decorated her dress in a pattern of pain, a drawing of doom. If I pushed her any further, I'd break her spirit and I didn't want to do that just yet. There was no fun in playing with lifeless puppets. No, they needed to have some fire burning inside of them, something they still held on to. Something they still had to lose.

"That will suffice for now," I told Halim, knowing that if I had Jamila flogged, the two women could potentially bond over their pain. And I wouldn't take that chance. No, if there was still a sliver of trust and affection left, this would smash it to pieces. Aliyah's resentment would grow every time the wounds and scars twinged in pain, every time she saw Jamila walk without a blemish on her skin. The constant searing on her back would keep her from recognising the scars on Jamila's soul.

This would destroy everything. And to make sure that Aliyah didn't associate her rage with me, I had Halim to make it all worse.

"It's time to leave," I commanded, brushing the dust from my dress and getting ready to head out of the dungeon. The heavy air was catching my breath and I was sure the dampness wasn't good for my skin. With shaking hands, Jamila crawled over to Aliyah to comfort her. I hid my grin and clacked my tongue. "No, not her. She stays."

Three pairs of questioning eyes stared at me. One pair filled with pain and exhaustion, one pair with sadness and desperation, one with lust and desire. I pointed at the one with sadness. "Jamila, we are leaving."

"W-What about her?" she whispered, her voice barely audible over the soft sobs of the bound woman. The sound of Halim's belt drew all our attention and I knew it wouldn't take long for him to burst out of his seams.

Jamila's eyes widened but before she could protest, I spoke. "You can leave with me or you can watch."

Another impossible choice.

"Please, I can't... I can't," my handmaiden whimpered, more tears spilling from her eyes. Pathetic.

"Jamila, don't leave me," Aliyah begged, finally thrashing against her constraints. With every step Halim took, she protested harder. A menacing grin contorted his face and while I never stayed behind, I had a pretty good idea of what he did to the chained victims in the dungeon. And from Aliyah's panicked cries, she knew too.

"Please, don't let him do this, please." She fought against the chains, the rope digging into her skin even more. I could tell from the reddened patches that this must've been hurting like a bitch. The two women exchanged exasperated looks and from Aliyah's muffled pleas, I knew what she wanted. She wanted Jamila to save her, but that wasn't about to happen. There was nothing my handmaiden could do to stop this.

"I'm sorry," Jamily whispered, shattering the sliver of hope dancing in Aliyah's eyes. I beckoned for my handmaiden and with her head hanging down like a tail between her legs, she followed as we left Aliyah in the dark with her worst nightmare. Her last cry almost traveled outside as I slammed the dungeons shut. Halim would deal with her, just like he always did. Perfect.

I turned to Jamila, staring in her traumatised eyes. This was the harshest punishment I dealt her and nothing compared to the personal whippings she received in the past. "Don't ever disappoint me again," I smiled sweetly, yet the threat was crystal clear.

Obediently, Jamila nodded. "I understand, Your Highness. Forgive me, Your Highness."

"All is forgotten." I stretched my arms, the muscles in my back twinging from the stress. "I believe a bath is in order. Jamila."

My handmaiden nodded hastily, scurrying away as fast as she could. It would take a while before she relaxed around me again, but I quite liked having her all tense and skittish. It made her all the better at her tasks.

I breathed in the floral air and enjoyed the delicate scent dancing in my nostrils. From across the courtyard, a flicker of green drew my attention and I paused in my step. Cautiously, I scanned around for any onlookers or unwanted bystanders but I didn't find anyone. And yet, with every step I took, I could swear someone was watching me. I was sure of it.

A breeze of air brushed through the patio and a glint of gold blinded me temporarily. Quickly, I darted up the balcony, never taking my eyes off a potted plant on the opposite side of the courtyard. The seconds ticked by as I waited with ragged breath in the shadows that enwrapped me. As expected, the bushes shook and muffled steps clacked on the stone floor. I didn't see the person leaving, but I had an idea of who had been watching me.

Jade.

Chapter 8. Weapon

A BREEZE OF FRESH AIR brushed through the flowers and the scent danced through the open window into my chambers. The gentle rays of the sun warmed my skin and with a soft buzz, the world came back to life.

Ah. Morning.

I slid out of my satin sheets and the soft carpet tickled the soles of my feet as I moved to the basin. A kind face greeted me as I sat down in front of the mirror and I shook my head in amusement. I had gotten really good at lying, so good my reflection almost fooled me.

I dug inside myself, behind the defences and lies I put up, into the depths of me. A wicked grin tugged up the corner of my lips and a playful glimmer danced in my eyes.

There I was. Now that face suited the real me. It was almost a shame I couldn't show it to the world. The world wouldn't understand. They weren't ready for me. Not yet.

A soft knock pulled me out of my thoughts and like dust in the wind, my grin vanished without leaving a trace. I brushed the wrinkles from my nightgown and straightened my slender shoulders.

"Come in," I called, immediately greeted with Jamila's face. The dark circles under her eyes told me she hadn't slept well.

The redness around her nose were a clear sign she'd been crying. Yes, she felt her punishment well.

"Good morning," I smiled, pretending last night hadn't happened. I would never bring it up and my handmaiden knew the consequences of mentioning it. She wasn't that stupid. I hid a small cough in my hand, planting the first seeds to my deceit.

"Good morning, Your Royal Highness. Did you have a good night's rest?" Despite the visible strain in her voice, she managed to sound almost cheery. She was a good liar, but not as good as me.

Without gracing her with a response, I waved my hand so she'd start my usual morning ritual. Carefully, Jamila massaged the silky almond cream into my skin and the nutty scent brought the room to life. I did love this smell. It was delicate, memorable, modest. The perfect disguise.

"Jamila."

"Yes, Your Royal Highness?" Concern flashed across her expression and it pleased me having her this attentive and skittish.

"I'm afraid I'll have to cancel my appointment with His Serene Highness. Do give him my sincerest apologies and please, let him know he is more than welcome to venture into the beautiful wilds."

"But, Your Highness... The complete royal entourage of Liechtenstein has gathered for the exploration."

I glared at Jamila, not appreciative of her protest. "Then his royal entourage can accompany him."

"Your Royal Highness, I ran into Zon this morning. He let me know that your brother, His Royal Highness Oumar, will be joining the entourage."

"Zon?" I asked, while admiring my long lashes framing a set of deep brown eyes.

"The new advisor to the Sultan."

"Ah." So Father got another lackey to 'advise' him. I knew what happened to the ones which didn't have advice that matched his opinion anyway. "Why is he following Oumar around?"

"He seems to have taken a shining to the crown prince." Jamila brushed an ivory comb through my hair and wove it into a beautiful braid. I did love having so many mirrors around me.

"So if Oumar is joining the tour, does that mean Princess Jade is accompanying them?" I asked casually, controlling my voice to constrain any hint of curiosity.

"No, Princess Jade is staying inside the palace. She expressed interest in the lustrous gardens."

"I see. Thank you, Jamila. You may leave now." I waved my hand dismissively and drew my attention back to my reflection. That was certainly a lot more interesting than my silly handmaiden.

"But... Your Royal Highness... They're all waiting for you to grace them with your presence?" she asked meekly, clearly scared to take any initiative on her own. At least she learned something from her punishment, but I had no need for a servant who needed hand-holding.

"And I told you I will not be attending. Do you know your task or do I need to spell it out for you?" I asked sweetly, yet I filled my words with poison.

"Of course not, Your Royal Highness. Certainly, Your Royal Highness. At once, Your Royal Highness," Jamila stuttered, exiting the room hastily without another word of protest. Good.

From my chambers, I had a perfect view of the gazebo. Even from this distance, I saw the glint of the sun reflected in his gold hair. I couldn't hear the words Jamila whispered to the servants, but from the disappointed look on Franz' face, I knew she relayed the message well. Perfect. That should give me some time to talk to Jade without the shielded words and veiled masks.

With a satisfied feeling bubbling up in my gut, I watched the concession come to life and the two princes marched down the lustrous greens towards their adventure. Men... They sure loved to play with their shiny guns. How frivolous, there was nothing more boring than a gun. One shot and it was all over.

No, I liked a different kind of weapon. An invisible one, untraceable, untouchable. The kind that haunted men and frightened children. A power only destined for the greatest on earth, an authority never to be challenged. A weapon only I could wield.

And I knew just the victim. Attracted by another golden glimmer, my eyes followed a slender figure weaving through the maze of flowerbeds. Now that the boys were away, the girls could play. And play with Jade I would.

Hastily, I draped my favourite scarf around my shoulders and with ragged breath, tip-toed down the heavy staircase. At this time of day, most of the guards were still on their way to their posts and it'd give me the perfect window of opportunity to mingle with Jade.

The grass bent under my feet as I rushed through the gardens with vigour. It wasn't very ladylike, but I didn't care. I wanted every second I could get with Jade, wanted every moment until I figured out what was beneath her perfectly sculpted mask.

"Princess Zafira. You surprise me," Jade said without even turning around to face me. I brushed my robes down and regained my composure. I didn't want to come to her like a panting dog, now that would truly be ungraceful.

"Forgive me for the intrusion, but you intrigue me, Princess Jade," I replied, my stomach clenching uncomfortably from the formalities. Last time, we established some more informal connection and I didn't want to move backwards. No, I wanted her to trust me, to confide in me, to bare her soul to me. And when she did, I'd crush her under my foot like a cockroach.

"Camille, you can go." Jade waved her hand in a way I recognised and one of her servants pardoned herself gracefully. Ah, that was the reason for the official titles.

As soon as Camille was out of hearing distance, Jade turned to me and smiled. "Zafira."

"Jade."

"How unexpected. I heard you excused yourself out of the hunt and yet, you grace me with your presence."

I flashed her a conspiring grin, some of my true nature dancing to the surface. "It was my humble opinion it'd be best to let the men play with their guns."

"Is that so," Jade said back, her own lips twitching up into a dazzling smile. She really was stunning and even I couldn't deny that. It was just a fact.

"And it gives us some time to get better acquainted," I added, gesturing at the Summer Resort. For a moment, I stared into Jade's bright green eyes and found myself reflected in the glimmer. I recognised myself in the endless depths and it had nothing to do with my reflection. She was... different. Unusual. There was something about her that lit up a small part of my brain, a twisted part that I hardly got to explore. And I wasn't about to pass up on this chance.

Chapter 9. Gardens

WITH JADE ACCOMPANYING me, we left the gardens behind us and moved to the coolness of the Summer Resort. With the rustic walls and the small windows, it was the perfect place to shield us from the harsh sunlight peeking through the deck of clouds.

"Finally alone," Jade remarked as she swung the heavy doors shut behind us. The rusty hinges shrieked loudly and with a thud, she sealed us off from the outside world. Perfect.

"Completely alone." I nodded, slowly pulling my scarf down so the gentle breeze could brush over my exposed shoulders.

"We can finally drop all the pretenses."

My stomach tightened under her alluring gaze and I drew in a sharp breath. Was this the moment when she'd tell me all about her dark little secrets? Oh, how I couldn't wait to hear all the naughty thoughts running through her head.

"To be completely honest with you..." Jade leaned in closer, her breath clashing against my skin. A shiver ran down my spine as I prepared for her confession. Maybe I'd get another glimpse of her real self.

"Yes?" I breathed, hoping not to break the spell we seemed to be under. I didn't want her to move away, no I just wanted her to come closer. Much closer.

"I hate the royal life."

"What?" My head snapped back in surprise and I stared in her green eyes with confusion. Was that really her dark secret? Was that all? That couldn't be all?

"Speaking with formal words all the time is really an annoyance. Every now and then... I wish I could..." Jade looked over her shoulder, as if to check we truly were alone. With a whisper, she drew me back in and her scent wafted up in my face.

Orchids. She smelled like orchids and vanilla. How utterly seductive and alluring. Almost irresistible.

"You wish you could what?" I asked softly, leaning into the web she weaved. If I knew it was a web, I wouldn't get caught in her traps. I just needed her to believe I was.

"Sometimes I wish I could swear," she admitted, her hot breath tickling my earlobe. She was close, much closer than I'd let any stranger come, and yet... It didn't feel wrong. It was exhilarating, like pure magic coursing untainted through my body. What if I calculated wrong? What if I got caught? How close could I let her come until it was too late to pull away? The risk I was taking was beyond exciting. It was my favourite game of playing chicken and I hadn't felt this alive in months or even years.

She really was the perfect victim. And I would go along with everything she said, until she believed with every bone of her body that I was a harmless little girl.

"Swearing? Could you provide me with an example?" I replied, making sure to calm the adrenaline powering through my veins.

"Fuck. Shit. Wanker," Jade breathed, her eyes lighting up with every word that'd leave a royal court in absolute devastation. This wasn't proper, it was nowhere near proper.

And I loved it.

"Asshole. Twat. Cunt face," I summed up, my breath catching in the back of my throat. I sounded excited and I almost felt it too. Being around Jade was exhilarating and I could almost believe I was a clueless princess being caught in the web of a rebellious seductress. Was this how it felt to be the victim? Was this the other side of the coin?

"Bloody hell." Jade circled around me like a vulture around prey. Her pink lips brushed across the shell of my ear and I felt tempted to lean back into her.

"What the fuck," I replied, a shiver running down my spine. She thought she was the one spinning a web, but silly her, she hadn't got a clue I was actually drawing her in. I was letting her come this close, just so the betrayal and deceit would be all the worse. Oh, it would devastate her to be played.

"Shithead," she murmured, the tone of her voice not matching the crudity of her words at all. No, it was silky smooth and alluring, almost tempting enough to give into the temptation.

"Suck my dick," I supplied, earning a soft giggle from the blonde. Unlike all the other grins and smiles she'd given me, this one sounded different. Lighter. Free. Honest. It felt genuine. Maybe the true Jade wasn't the devious mastermind that I hoped her to be. Maybe she was just a real good soul, caged in a role she had to play?

That was... disappointing. Or was it? I couldn't work out how that made me feel.

"You truly are something else, Zafira," she purred in my ear, her tongue clacking seductively. No, this couldn't be an innocent woman, there was no way. I couldn't fall into the trap of believing that. She was twisted, just like me. And this, this was a game to her. She was trying to trap me in her lies, in the same way I loved playing with people. But I saw right through her and when she expected it the least, I'd turn the tables on her. Oh hell I would.

Another whiff of orchids danced past me and the floral scent elicited something from deep within me. I turned around to face the beautiful blonde and let her green eyes peer deep inside mine. She wouldn't find anything I didn't want to show anyway.

She waved a little fly away and her hand fluttered past my cheek, her fingers soft and gentle. I shivered as one of her hands found my waist, caught off guard by her audacity. Nobody had ever touched me without my permission and I could have her flogged for this.

Instead, I wetted my lips and allowed her to step even closer to me. Her hand slid from my waist to the small of my back and I knew she could feel the goosebumps scattered across my skin.

"Are you okay?" she asked, surprisingly thoughtful. Robbed from any words, I just nodded. This was a game, just a game. That was the only reason I allowed her so close. That was why I would let her—

My thoughts were cut off by the softest pair of lips brushing over mine. My breath caught in the back of my throat and I disappeared into the scent of orchids and vanilla. With a tenderness I hadn't expected from her, she moved her lips against mine, the friction shooting electricity up and down my spine. Magic. The only word I managed to find for the sensation of being properly kissed was magic.

Whatever her reasons were, whatever mine were, they vanished in the intensity of the kiss and the dance our tongues engaged in. Skin against skin, lips on lips, player against player. It was *on*.

Chapter 10. Farah

ELECTRICITY SPARKED between me and Jade, the tension setting my body ablaze in a whirlwind of lust and desire. I tilted my head back, suppressing the urge to take over and blow the cover I was playing as the innocent girl. I couldn't risk her realising what kind of monster I held deep inside. No, that wouldn't bode well. Not yet.

For now, I'd let her kiss me and pretend to be all dazzled and enamoured by it. I'd let her believe she had this effect on me. It was fake, everything I felt was just pretend. It just had to be.

Her slender fingers traced lines across my neck and I wondered whether she'd try and choke me. If it were the other way around, I would surely be tempted.

Her tongue brushed past my bottom lip and I groaned involuntarily. She was a good kisser.

No, she was a great kisser. Passionate, yet tender. Both thorough and playful, a perfect mix of gentle and rough. A kiss worth melting for.

Not like I could melt, no... This sensation, it was just me experiencing the lie. The excitement came from knowing I was drawing her closer, deeper into a web she wouldn't be able to escape. A perfect trap. And she'd fall for it, oh she would. She wouldn't see any of it coming and when it was far too late to return, I would make her fall.

In the trap. Not for me. In the trap.

I curled my arms around her slender waist, the scent of orchids dancing around us in the breeze. The smell of the summer air complemented her distinct fragrance in a melody I could only describe as perfect harmony.

I'd been right. Jade truly was something else.

She parted her lips and pressed her leg between mine. A twinge shot through my core and I refrained from pulling her harder into me. I wouldn't let the lust clouding my head blow my cover, but how I wanted to let the monster come out to devour the beautiful woman in my arms. Maybe next time.

No, not maybe. I would make sure there was a next time. I would make her want me like she hadn't wanted anyone else before. Her head would spin, her heart pound, her soul ache. The more she desired me, the more it would hurt when I broke the illusions and revealed the lies. The more she lusted after me, the more she'd miss my delicate touch, my hot breath on her skin, my hand between her legs. When I was done with her, this powerful and majestic woman would be reduced to a mess, void of any trust or hope.

With the long game in mind, I enjoyed Jade's kiss for another moment longer before gently pushing her away. A confused look chased away the lust in her eyes and it was quite adorable. Like a puppy.

"You okay?" she breathed, the softness of her words surprisingly gentle.

"Yes, I just needed a moment," I whispered back, spinning another lie. It really was a lie. It wasn't possible that she was actually affecting me. Nobody had affected me in my entire life. People just didn't do that.

I stared into Jade's deep green eyes and softly whimpered as she curled her fingers in my hair. There was a tenderness to her strokes that had me wondering how genuine our connection was. Maybe there was such thing as two rotten peas in a pod?

Or maybe I'd already made her crazy about me, yearning for my touch, desperate for my attention. Maybe she was just as gullible as all the other women after all.

The beauty clacked her tongue and stole a quick peck from my lips. Any seductiveness in her eyes had made place for a nonchalant look as she stepped back.

"I'm afraid it's time for one of my regimes. If you'd excuse me?"

I bit my tongue as she pretended it was her who decided the moment was over. But I couldn't show my hand by pointing that out, no, I had to play along in the polite royal manner I always did.

"Naturally. I've been keeping you too long," I spoke, bowing ever so slightly.

"Thank you. It was an absolute *pleasure* to have you here," she smiled, some of the earlier playfulness reappearing in her voice.

"The pleasure was all mine." I refrained from winking at her, but I was sure my tone reflected my sentiment. After all, she knew what I meant. Without looking back at her, I strode out of the Summer Resort. I silenced the flutter in my chest and ignored all the servants staring at me walking through the gardens on my own. I forgot I ditched all my handmaidens, but now I looked ridiculous.

"Your Royal Highness, let me help you." Farah ran to my side and popped out an umbrella. The shade immediately soothed the not-unpleasant glow that the sun left on my skin. I studied the woman, the stench of greed wafting off of her. She was clearly trying to get a leg up and while I appreciated ambition, I didn't tolerate it. She wasn't here to please me, no she wanted to get out of the dump she grew up in and serving me was the fastest way to do it. But I had no use for maidens like that. But she was in luck. After my encounter with Jade, I wanted to play.

"Farah, what do you think the position of head handmaiden entails?" I asked slyly, masking my true intentions.

She gasped and a list of tasks rattled from her mouth. Some accurate, some highly inaccurate. But that didn't matter, I just needed her to believe she'd be perfect. And of course, she did.

"Between you and me, Your Royal Highness, I think Jamila is slacking."

"What makes you say that?" I asked coyly, innocently. As if I didn't understand that was trying to make her look bad.

"She really messed up with that Aliyah, that other girl. And now that Aliyah isn't here anymore, the position is open again but she doesn't want to tell you."

"Go on," I smiled, ignoring the palace guards as the shade of the palace fell on me. The stone tiles clacked under my heels as I retreated to my chambers. Farah trotted behind me, the umbrella still over my head. What a stupid goose. She needed to be taught a lesson.

With the frustrations bubbling up in my stomach, I turned the corner and rerouted to the barracks. I didn't often visit them directly, but I was in need of one of my tools.

"After Aliyah received her punishment, that she clearly deserved, she spent two days moping in the kitchens and then just disappeared. We heard that she fell in love with one of the palace guards and ran off with him."

"Oh my goodness," I gasped fakely, refraining from rolling my eyes. I didn't know exactly what Halim did to the young woman, but whisking her off her feet wasn't it.

"Yes, and to top that off, Jamila is looking for a replacement and hoping you won't notice!"

I stopped so abruptly, Farah almost tripped over my feet. She coughed loudly to cover up her mistake and quickly patted down my dress. Multiple footsteps sounded through the hallway and Jamila and a handful of my other servants came running towards me.

"Your Royal Highness, forgive me. You asked for privacy, but I didn't realise you already left the Summer Resort."

"Be still, Jamila. Leave us."

A smug grin stretched across Farah's face and I beckoned for her to follow me. Even from the corners of my eyes, I could see her mouth words to my handmaiden. She was getting comfortable, too comfortable. But that was exactly what I wanted.

"Send for Halim," I ordered a random guard, not even waiting for his response. I didn't have to. Within these walls, my word was law.

I turned at Farah's gittish face and couldn't wait to paint it with devastation. She would be fun to break.

"I seek advice," I lied, roping her further into a false sense of security.

"It would be my honour."

It would be indeed.

Chapter 11. Punishment

I ALLOWED HER TO COME a little closer than I liked and whispered in her ear. "What sort of punishment would you see fit for a... handmaiden that doesn't know her place?" Her ego would prevent her from ever thinking I meant her. No, her stupid mind would immediately jump to Jamila, but that was just what I wanted.

"My goodness, such insubordination should be gravely punished."

"I believe you are correct," I egged her on, guiding her towards her own downfall. "What punishment would fit such an error in judgment?"

Her eyes lit up and she couldn't hide the gleeful smile stretching across her face. "Your highness, you flatter me with your trust. If it was up to me, I wouldn't want to be too harsh, just make it so... She wouldn't be able to serve anymore."

"That's very creative," I complimented, drawing her in with flattery. She beamed and practically bounced next to me. I could smell her greed and I couldn't wait to turn it into regret. I found Halim waiting for me at the dungeons and from his pervy smile, he knew exactly what he was here for.

"Do you remember the dungeons, Farah?" I asked, wondering when exactly the truth would sink in.

"Yes! Is Jamila waiting for us down here?"

It was almost hard to contain my laughter, what a stupid goose this one was. I nodded at Halim and he swung the dungeon doors open. The dust fluttered up in the sunlight as I led Farah down. It wasn't a place I liked spending time in, but it was soundproof and no windows meant no accidental onlookers.

We crossed the threshold and the emergency lights immediately jumped on. The glimmer reflected in his dark eyes and the moment the doors fell shut, the monster came out. His expression changed right in front of me. I imagined if I didn't know him, I wouldn't want to meet him in an alleyway. But his twisted desires weren't my concern. I was his master and he was the bloodhound I set loose.

"Where's Jamila?" Farah asked, her voice betraying the first sliver of doubt.

"She's not coming."

The blank look in her eyes quickly turned to fear and her face fell as her mind connected the dots. Horror flashed across her face as she darted backwards. She shot a helpless look at Halim but he wouldn't come to her aid. No, he was the thing she should be running from.

"Your Royal Highness, I think there has been a mistake..."

I gently fanned myself. "Are you implying that I'm wrong?"

"No, of course not, no... I'm just... What's he doing? What are you doing?" she screeched, swatting at Halim. He grabbed her by the wrists, a deranged look passing through his eyes.

"Here, here, be silent, little one," he grinned.

"Your Royal Highness, please!"

"What advice did you give me again?" I asked, pretending like I didn't remember. She screamed and clawed at Halim. He growled and loosened his grip on her for a moment. The panic made itself clear as she called for more help and scratched the door, but they were firmly locked. I made sure of it.

"Please, stop this. I take it all back, I'm sorry. Please!" she begged, the desperation growing with every passing moment.

"Okay then." Expectation grew in her eyes and I let it. I wanted her to believe she could get out of this, I wanted her on the edge of insanity. Hope filled her voice as she fell to her knees, crying and begging. I took a step back, not wanting to be touched by such a pathetic person.

I turned to Halim and nodded. "Let's get started."

Farah's scream could've cut through bones as I shattered all her hope and trust in me. She pleaded all the way up to the same restraints I had Jamila in last time. Many women and men before them had taken their place but not many had left alive.

"I can't remember what you said before... If a servant is insubordinate, they should be punished. Is that correct?"

"No, please... I didn't mean to—"

"Didn't mean it? So you lied to me?"

"Of course not, I would never lie to you. Please, Your Highness, spare me. Have mercy."

"Oh, I will show you mercy." I turned to my bloodhound and smiled. "Halim, what is your favourite tool?"

"The whip, Your Highness," he answered, his voice filled with boyish excitement.

I nodded. "Not today. Sword."

His face fell, but he obeyed like a good toy. Farah screamed again at the sight of the metal glinting as he unsheathed a sword. He waved it front of his face a couple of times, clearly trying to install fear in the bound woman.

"Your advice to punish a servant was so she couldn't be able to serve anymore. I wonder how we can make that true today..."

"Don't servants need their hands to serve?" Halim chipped in, his voice shaking in anticipation.

"That's a good point," I smiled, studying Farah's expressions. Her face was white from fear and the horror was already drawing hard lines of worry. Soon she wouldn't have tears left to cry and no voice left to scream.

"May I, Your Royal Highness?" My bloodhound stepped closer to Farah, the sword trembling in his hand. He placed it softly on her wrist, just behind the shackle. The woman thrashed against her bounds, her wails echoing across the dungeon. She was so loud, it was annoying me.

I bent down and leant towards her ear. "If you don't stop screaming, I will have Halim cut off your fingers one by one and use them to gag you," I smiled politely, enjoying the immediate petrification of her. "That's better."

"Aww, I liked the screaming," Halim pouted, looking disappointed with her silence. I ignored him and took in the sight in front of me. He got off on the struggle and crying, but that didn't really do anything for me.

I loved the moment they gave up, the exact time their will broke and they became lifeless puppets. There was nothing more exhilarating than watching someone die before they actually did. And she was almost there.

"Halim, take her hand."

Farah's eyes widened, a string of whimpers escaping her mouth. She was terrified, beyond terrified, but she was staying silent. The fear of what might happen was still worse than what actually happened to her so far. But that was about to change.

Gently, I stroked her cheek and smiled. "Remember what I said."

I stepped back before the blood spattered against Halim's pants and the iron scent filled the dungeon. Farah broke her silence with a scream that would haunt anyone's dreams, but not mine. This was just a noise like any other.

"Oh fuck, oh fuck, oh fuck!'

First, there was just pain. The shock pulled all the colour out of her face but she hadn't seen it yet. With no hand attached to her arm, it slipped out of the shackle and she held it up to the light. Waves of blood pulsated out of the arteries and rapidly collected in puddles at her knees.

"Oh my god, my hand. You took my hand!" she called as she stared at the stump.

Disbelief. It always took a second or two for before it sank in that this wasn't some awful nightmare, that this wasn't a prank gone wrong. Two seconds before they understood this was their new reality.

Farah's eyes traveled from her maimed arm to her severed hand on the ground and it clicked. Her screams grew silent and her eyes rolled back into her skull.

Loss of consciousness. The body's natural defense mechanism against trauma and the least enjoyable to watch.

"Bandage her."

Reluctantly, Halim put the blood-stained sword down and revealed an emergency kit from the shadows. Expertly, he threaded the needle and sewed up the stump with a few stitches. It certainly helped that he was training to be a doctor. With the raw flesh tied together, he wound some cloth around the dismembered arm and applied pressure to stop her from bleeding out. With a gentleness you'd expect from a physician, he pushed a whole shot of morphine in her system and nodded to himself.

"That should take care of her pain and stop the bleeding."

"Excellent." Her dying in this dungeon would bring along annoying complications and I didn't really want that. No, I wanted to play more but she *had* to pass out.

Halim adjusted his pants and from the extra touches and strokes he gave her, I knew he was having a hard time controlling his urges. "Your Royal Highness, may I?"

There was an irony in him asking my consent while violating hers, but that really wasn't any of my concerns. I prefered him exploring his darkest desires on targets I chose than having him go rampant in the palace.

"Be my guest."

Not wanting to risk being caught waiting outside of the dungeon, I dusted off one of the chairs and seated myself.

Halim dropped his pants and his member sprung free. Even from this far, I could see the light glint on the purple head. He licked his lips, his eyes clouded with animalistic lust. Impatiently, he grabbed Farah's robes, ready to tear them off.

"Don't rip her dress," I scolded, not amused that I needed to remind him that the women needed to look halfway decent when they left after their punishment. His face fell, but he didn't dare challenge my command. Carefully, he pushed her clothes aside and moaned at the sight. He grunted loudly as he penetrated her, his thighs slapping against her buttocks. With loud groans, he used the unconscious woman for his own twisted desires and I rolled my eyes. Pathetic.

"Make it quick," I yawned, not particularly enjoying the sound of him moaning. I'd have prefered to try a different way of waking her up, but if he became too pent up, he couldn't focus. Men...

The sound of flesh meeting flesh echoed through the dungeon and from his accelerated groaning, it became apparent he was close to finishing. After all the practice, it still surprised me how little stamina he had.

As he thrust inside her for the last spurts, her eyes fluttered open and some colour returned to her face. It took her a moment to realise she was still bound in the dungeons and another couple of seconds for her to understand what was happening. Surprisingly agitated, she bucked against Halim, hoping to throw him off.

From the grin on his face, it was clear this was his favourite part.

"Yes, little one, fight me," he hissed, his fingers curling into her waist. He quickened his pace and slammed deeper into her, spurred on by her protest. She thrashed against him, struggling to get away from his abuse, but it was no use. The shackle would keep her right where he wanted her.

With her last hope, she looked up at me. "Please..."

Excruciatingly slow, I got up from my seat and walked towards her. Hope shimmered in her eyes and I clicked my tongue. She really wasn't learning.

I crouched down next to the desperate figure and patted her cheek. I touched the metal clasp around her wrist, brushing one finger over the shackle. Did she really think I was going to free her? People were so easy to toy with.

With a little laugh, I shook my head and walked away from Farah. The desperation sank in and the final acceptance arrived. Instead of fighting the abuse, she grew lifeless and the fire behind her eyes went out.

I studied the exchange, hoping it would teach me more about humanity and their ever growing desires. Hoped it would help me understand what made a person hold on, what they lived for, what made them tick. I wanted to know why they cried, what they held dear, how they loved. Because all those things were foreign to me.

I dusted off my robe and nudged Halim. "We're done here."

"I'm close."

"Just make sure to dispose of her properly. I have no need for her anymore."

His last grunts followed me as I left the dungeon, trusting Halim to clean up after his little escapade. None of my servants had shown back up after their punishment, so I left him to it.

The sun fell on my skin again as there was nobody to hold the shade. Oh well, it was quite pleasant after being in the cool dungeon. If I hadn't been a princess, I'd have whistled a little tune. What a beautiful day.

Playing with Farah had been fun, but it didn't scratch the itch I had ever since Jade entered the palace. This was just a little appetiser. The real fun had only just begun and this time, I'd go directly to the source.

Chapter 12. Shackles

ANOTHER BANQUET, HOW boring. I smiled politely at Franz across the table and dreaded another meeting with him. Apparently, he was quite insistent on me joining him for the next event as I missed the previous one.

The mint danced on my palate as I took a sip from my refreshing beverage. The chili from the tagine prickled my nose and danced through the air. At least our chef was decent.

I took a small bite as I caught Jade's gaze from across the hall. She smiled behind her fork, her eyes lighting up. She whispered something to her brother and pushed her chair back. Without breaking eye contact, she excused herself from the table.

This was my chance to get her back. Nobody dismissed me from my own palace, not even Princess Jade. I beckoned Jamila and nudged at the princess. "Tell the servants to guide Princess Jade to my private lavatory."

"As you wish, Your Royal Highness." She whispered something in another woman's ear and I watched her rush over to the other side of the hall. Pleased, the young servant steered her towards my chambers.

Silently, I counted out twenty seconds and then motioned Jamila to escort me to the lavatory. Without haste, I took the time to thank Father for the meal and made my way to my wing.

"Stay," I commanded, making my handmaidens wait in the hallway. I didn't want them around when I talked to Jade. Jamila nodded and opened the doors to my quarters. My heels echoed on the stone floor as I caught the alluring blonde waiting for me at the seating area.

"Zafira."

"Jade."

"I believe I owe it to you for allowing me to use your private powder room," she smiled, her lips curling up in an alluring smile.

"That is correct."

"You have my thanks."

I waved her gratitude away and leant against one of the seats. "Did the banquet not please you?"

A short laugh fell from her pink lips and Jade shook her head, her blonde locks dancing around her face. "It was perfectly alright, but I enjoy some privacy after dinner."

"You have all the privacy here that you need," I gestured. "These are my personal quarters and my handmaiden won't allow anyone in."

"Your handmaiden's help is appreciated."

"Jamila does her job well."

"That she does." Jade stretched her neck, the muscles flexing in her slender body. "I do prefer silence over such crowded banquets."

"I can understand that," I said while stepping closer to her, making sure to sway my hips seductively. I caught her eyes and stared into the deep green. There was something about her, something that even drew me in. Maybe this would help me understand what it was to desire something or someone.

"But your company is much appreciated," she added softly, both her tone and the look in her eyes changing. The predatory glimmer made way for an unexpected vulnerability. A little thrown off, I paused and admired the woman in front of me.

With her mesmerising green eyes and polished features, she was undeniably beautiful. She was beyond that. It was easy to forget the wickedness lying behind the perfection.

I trailed my finger over her arm, drawing goosebumps across her skin. Without breaking eye contact, she leant in and snaked her arm around my waist. A timeless moment passed between us before she gently pressed her lips on mine. The excitement coursing through me wasn't comparable to anything else I'd experienced before. Not with the thrill of robbing someone of their innocence, of their hope, trust, love, life.

Kissing Jade was something entirely else and I didn't want it to stop. I intertwined my hand with hers and pulled her closer into me. A murmur escaped from her lips as I deepened the kiss, her tongue wrapping around mine. Passion flamed up in my stomach as it awoke a lust buried deep inside of me.

"Your company isn't so bad either," I breathed, eliciting a chuckle from the blonde. She brought my hands up with hers and guided my body backwards until it met a wall. I gasped as she propped her leg up between mine and hit a sensitive spot. I could have her flogged for this indecent behaviour, but instead I pulled her to me.

With lust and fire raging through my veins, I threaded one of my hands in her hair and flipped her so she was pressed against the wall. Jade moaned into the kiss and it awoke my primal instincts. I wanted her, with everything that I had, I wanted her to submit.

I pulled out of the kiss to take a breath and studied her expression. With her green eyes a couple of shades darker than before, I was confident I had an effect on her. I just dreaded to see what kind of effect she was having on me.

My mind barely registered where her hands were roaming. I bet this wasn't what Father had in mind when he invited them over for a peace treaty. Oh, I would make peace with this woman and then after she trusted me, set heaven on fire.

Possessively, I dug my fingers into her hips and ground myself against her. The blonde whimpered, some of her composure breaking. There was a desperation in her touches, one that only I could satisfy. I trailed kisses down the side of her face, taking advantage of the haze of lust to push her chin upwards. Smugly, I nipped at her neck, almost breaking the skin as I left a reddening mark. Her head rolled back and I took it as an invitation to continue. I slipped my hand between her and the wall, looking for the zipper to her dress.

She arched her back and I relaxed a little. Wrong move. With the agility of a wild cat, she flipped me and once again, I found myself trapped between the heat of her body and the cold wall. Without waiting for permission, she pushed my dress to the side and electricity sprang to my skin as she touched a part of my thigh that not many had seen or been allowed to touch. And yet, here she was, taking what wasn't hers, just because she could. A growl rolled from her lips as she attacked my neck with demanding kisses and possessive nips.

Angrily, I found myself tingling and whimpering under her touch, my body reacting to her involuntarily. This wasn't supposed to happen, I wasn't supposed to be under her spell. I wanted her under mine. That would teach her for dismissing me, for kissing me without permission, for making me want her. I was done playing the innocent girl around her, I wanted her to understand who she was dealing with, that she was playing with the hottest and most dangerous kind of fire. She would pay for making me feel this, this helpless, this out of control, this obsessed.

Between the string of kisses, I found the zipper to her dress and yanked it down. The metal shrieked, but it was no match for me. I peeled the fabric away and unclasped the bra obstructing me from getting what I wanted. *Her.*

Jade moaned against my neck, her hot breath tickling on the sensitive skin. Heat surged through my body all the way to my core and it was excruciatingly frustratingly sexy. Why did she have this effect on me and how could I make it stop? How could I make her submit to me?

Chapter 13. Lust

LUST RAGED THROUGH my mind, preventing me from thinking straight, from forming all the twisted plans. I pushed the haze back and tried to ignore the tingling between my legs.

If I couldn't get a hold over myself here, I needed to bring her somewhere I knew I could. My bedroom.

Yes, bring her to my battlefield. My comfort.

"Hang on," I gasped between her relentless assault on my senses. Instead of halting, she curled her fingers harder into my waist, peppering more kisses in my neck.

"Jade, hang on."

The blonde pulled back, her eyes shimmering with mischief. "Sorry, I didn't hear you," she grinned, not even bothering to cover up the lie. Determined not to let her get to me, I shrugged and weaseled out from the precarious position she had me trapped in. Her green eyes followed me across the room as I moved to the bedroom door. Opening it just wide enough so I could pass through, I paused to take in the moment.

I caught her gaze and smiled, almost innocently. The confusion in her eyes was truly beautiful and I basked in the shift of control. Now she was my plaything.

I managed to light five candles before Jade entered the room, her dress barely covering her. From the flicker passing through her eyes, I could tell the change had thrown her off her game. I imagined there hadn't been a living soul that'd managed to tell Jade to stop, but I did. I wasn't just a regular girl she could play with.

I sat down on my bed and stared lustfully at the blonde. I needed her to believe I craved her beyond all other things and it wasn't very hard to pretend this was my truth. There was hardly any pretending, but I would never let a living soul know she had a genuine effect on me. Not even her.

With a smirk, Jade moved her shoulder and the elegant dress cascaded down her body, exposing a true beauty. The fabric rustled as it fell to the floor, leaving a shell of the blonde on the tiles.

Painstakingly slow, foot for foot, she moved closer to me. Mesmerised with the curve of her waist and her swaying hips, my breath hitched in my throat. There was something both powerful and vulnerable about the way she approached me and I couldn't figure out if I was luring her or if she was chasing me. Maybe both were true.

Seductively, she crossed her arms and let her bra travel down her shoulders. She was so close, if I reached out, I could touch her. I wanted to. I needed to.

Surprised to find my hand trembling, I brushed my fingers softly over her stomach. Jade sucked in a breath and chuckled throatily, the dim light dancing in her dark eyes. Enchanted with her beauty, I took one last look at her before I extinguished out the candles. With the darkness, Jade fell into my bed and entangled herself with me. I stroked her naked back and temporarily wondered what it'd be like if we were two regular people. If I were capable of feeling, maybe Jade would be someone I could love.

Her hands traveled under my own dress and caressed the sensitive skin between my thighs. Her lips found mine and without the urgency from before, she kissed me. Thoroughly, completely, fully. I moaned into the embrace and wrapped my arms around her waist, wanting her impossibly closer. Yes, if I was a normal person, I could end up loving her.

But I wasn't. The darkness hid my devious grin as I flipped her on her back. I pressed my thigh between hers, temporarily flooding her mind with a haze of lust. I only needed a moment, two seconds of her being unguarded to lift her hands up and click them in the hidden restraints at either side of my bed.

"Relax," I breathed against her neck, trailing a patch of kisses across her collarbone.

"I am," Jade whispered back, her voice oddly calm. Almost as if she expected this. I had to admit, it wasn't my favourite way of taking control, but she was too dangerous. Even if binding her was a little cheat, it still got her where I wanted her. Underneath me in submission.

But then why didn't she look bothered? Even without proper lighting, I could make out her relaxed features. Did she not feel threatened?

I dragged my nails across her arm, hoping to make her realise the direness of her situation. She was naked and bound at my mercy, and I didn't know what mercy meant.

Teasingly, I drew circles around her perked nipples, avoiding any real contact or stimulation. The blonde stared at me, the control slipping out of her eyes with every circle. Gently at first, I rolled one of the pink buds between my fingers and rejoiced at the gasp I elicited from her. Faster than I usually did, I peppered kisses down her neck and wetted my lips as I made contact. She arched up from the bed, her excitement no longer a guessing matter. She sucked in her stomach as I drew a trail of kisses between her breasts, inching closer and closer to the last piece of clothing. The lace wasn't going to protect her for much longer. I hooked one finger inside the waistband and was met with surprisingly smooth skin. Jade whimpered softly as the cool air brushed between her thighs and I grinned against her skin.

"Relax," I said once more, opening her legs wider to expose her to me. Feeling a little cruel, I licked the inside of her thigh, closer and closer to her core. The scent of her arousal filled my nose and I almost wished I left some candles on so I could admire the sight of her.

She arched into me as I flicked my finger across her sensitive bud, the first real moan escaping her lips. Heaven. The sound was heavenly and I wanted to hear more, so much more. A little more urgent, I pressed my fingers down on her wetness and drew another groan from her.

"Don't stop," she mewled, her voice thick with desire.

"Ask me," I grinned, my fingers growing still. Desperately, she wiggled her hips in search of friction, but I wouldn't let her.

"Zafira..."

"I'm listening," I teased, stroking the inside of her thigh. She quivered against my touch, finally fighting against the constraints. "I can't hear you."

"Damn you," she spat, tugging harder on the chains.

"That's not very princess-like."

"I'm going to ki—"

I didn't let her finish her sentence. Instead, I abruptly nipped at her other thigh, not hard enough to break the skin, but I knew she'd have felt it. I slid my fingers through her folds, stealing the words from her mouth. Teasingly, I danced circles around her sensitive bud, applying enough pressure to fill her head with sinful thoughts of wanton and desire. The blonde moaned softly, the lust spilling from her lips. With every flick, every stroke, every slippery ministration, Jade grew more and more restless.

Just watching her fight against the chains and pleasure, powerless and helpless, sent chills down my spine. There was something beautiful and honest about submission. Her true nature exposed in front of my very eyes, just for me. And I basked in the knowledge that I had her body, her mind, her sanity in my hands.

I found her sensitive bundle of nerves with my thumb and used my other fingers to hit a spot deep inside of her. She gasped loudly, her green eyes rolling back into her skull with pleasure. She was getting close to the brink of release and the closer she came, the more panicked she seemed. I was stripping her of something, something she hadn't thought I was capable of taking. But I would. In this room, in this bed, I was God.

She tightened around my fingers, her moans more desperate than before. The urgency and intimacy of the moment set fire to me and I spurred her on, bringing her closer and closer to her release. Jade balled her fists, her hands clawing into the sheets. Her slender body bucked against my hand, her wetness coating my fingers. She was close, very close.

Her eyes blasted open and she filled the room with her scream. As far as the restraints allowed her, she shot up and stared at me, a deranged look flitting across her face. "Don't stop!"

Oops, did I stop? How mean of me. I drew small circles, never actually touching the bundle of nerves that would give Jade the release she so craved.

"Tell me what you want," I instructed, flicking my fingers over her wanton core to keep her highly stimulated but never enough that it pushed her over the edge.

Chapter 14. Begging

THE HATE SWIRLED IN her dark eyes as she thrashed against the chains. If looks could kill me, I'd be on my way to hell right now. The conflict carved deep lines in her beautiful face as I made her choose between control or release. Her call.

I curled my finger up, hitting the same spot I'd been stimulating and she quivered involuntarily.

"Am I stopping or starting again?"

"Fuck you."

"Stopping then." The moment I pulled my fingers away, Jade whimpered desperately. She wiggled her hips, grinding herself against the bed. Frustrated, she clenched her legs in a last attempt to satisfy her own need, but there was no use. With her hands bound safely above her head, there was only one person who could give her what she so desired.

"No, don't stop," she mewled, her whisper barely audible.

"I can't hear you," I grinned, walking my fingers over her thigh. Closer and closer, but never touching.

"Don't stop."

"Beg me," I commanded, the darkness rising from its cage. I got her right where I wanted.

Jade hesitated for a moment too long and I let my finger slip through her folds, slowly, teasingly. Like a promise of what was to come.

"Please," she whimpered, the plea music to my ears. This was what I loved. Total submission from someone that never submitted before.

That was all I needed. I pressed my thumb down on her sensitive bud and shoved my fingers deep inside of her, hitting all the right spots at once. Her legs fell open as wide as they possibly could and her moan vibrated through her whole body. Intoxicating. Addictive. I wouldn't be opposed to doing that again.

A loud knock pulled me out of the moment and frustrated, I called out. "Leave us!"

"Your Royal Highness, it's important," Jamila stressed from outside the door.

"It can wait!" Angered at the interruption, I curled my fingers up and applied even more pressure on Jade's wanton core. She mewled from the intensity, spurred on by the roughness. Good to know.

"I'm so sorry to disturb you, Your Highness, but Halim said it can't wait."

I froze. From Jade's frantic groans, I could tell she wasn't pleased with the sudden stop. She ground herself against my hand, trying to inflict the same pressure on herself. Annoyed, I pulled my hand away and left the blonde growling at the bed.

"This better be worth my time," I snarled, opening the door just a crack.

"Halim says he requires your presence immediately."

"Let him wait." I slammed the door shut, irritated by her interruption.

"He says it's about Farah?"

Damn it. I swung the door back open. "What about her?"

"He didn't specify, Your Highness. He just stressed how urgent this was."

"Fine." I tightened my dress and stared at the blonde in my bed. The way she was clawing and thrashing against her restraints was beautiful. Animalistic. Pure. "I'll be back."

"No, don't you dare leave me!"

"Behave while I'm gone," I joked, sniffing my fingers to get a whiff of her scent. Oh how I couldn't wait to come back to that and have a proper taste.

"Zafira, I'm serious. Don't you dare!"

"What are you going to do?" I laughed, quickly rinsing her off my hands. Yes, binding her had been a good choice.

"Damn it, come back here. I command—"

"You command me?" I bellowed, whipping the towel at her naked body. "You dare command me? You're in my country, in my palace, in my *bed*. You may be a princess where you come from, but in here, you are to satisfy my every need, every whim, every desire. Do I make myself clear?"

"Fuck you!" she spat, fire blazing behind her eyes. She was terrifying and part of me feared what she'd do the moment I took her chains off. Another part of me couldn't wait to find out.

"Suit yourself." I clicked my tongue, impressed she managed to draw some of my real self out and disappointed I let her. I smiled politely at Jamila, tempted to tell her nobody was allowed inside my chambers but that was redundant. Nobody was ever allowed inside, so specifying would just be ridiculous. She seemed rather curious, but luckily didn't ask any questions. Good servant.

"Halim is waiting for you at the west temple."

"Perfect." I didn't want to run through the palace, which would've aroused quite a bit of suspicion, but I hasted as quickly as I could through the halls. My handmaidens rushed behind me, their footsteps drawing even more attention to me. "Jamila, I have no need for you."

"But, Your Royal Highness..."

"Is that disobedience I hear?"

"No, of course not. As you wish. Your Royal Highness." She snapped at the rest of the maidens and they quickly scattered into the many doors and pathways. With a bow, my handmaiden turned backwards and left me to myself.

Rid of their annoying chatter, I followed the west corridor to the entrance of the temple. A hooded figure emerged from the shadows and quickly revealed Halim's face. The panic stretched across his features wasn't a good sign and I wondered what he could've possibly done to look this pained.

"Speak," I commanded, disgusted by his sniffling face.

"Your Highness, something has gone terribly wrong. When I returned for Farah—"

"Returned?"

"Yes, when I tried to leave, I noticed one of the guards at the gate."

"There shouldn't be any guards, you said the dungeons aren't on the roster."

Hamil wrung his hands, worry splayed across his face. "It shouldn't be, but I checked and the captain added it onto the schedule. It's guarded day and night now."

So my little torture place was no longer usable. That was a little annoying, but not a big problem. There were plenty of other hidden shelters and dungeons running under the palace grounds.

"So what about Farah?"

"Your Royal Highness, I don't know how it happened... When I returned, she was gone."

"Gone?" I asked sharply, glaring at the young man. I gave him one job and he failed?

"Yes, I don't know how. There was a guard all night."

"Was she still bound?"

"Yes! Someone must've helped her, but who knew we were even there?"

"Nobody," I said, but I knew the answer. There was only one person who'd been following me around from the shadows. Jade. She needed to be punished for her crime, and luckily, I knew just where to find her.

"Halim."

"Yes?"

"You've gravely disappointed me. Return to your quarters until I'm ready to deal with you."

Like a beaten dog, my bloodhound crawled back. "Yes, Your Royal Highness. At once, Your Royal Highness."

Not even taking the time to dismiss him further, I turned on my heels and rushed back to my chambers. I didn't care who saw me, this was too important. There was a reason Jade hadn't told the palace about Farah yet, she had something in mind and I wasn't going to like it.

I needed to deal with her for once and for good. No more time for playing, she was too dangerous. I couldn't have her loitering around in the palace, not with this kind of leverage over me. Damn it, I underestimated her!

She knew this, all of this while lying naked in my bed. It'd had been a distraction, a play. And I fell for it, hook, line, and sinker. Oh, the shame. The disgrace. I would make sure she paid, that she paid for this a million times with a million lives. After I was done with her, she'd be nothing but a shadow of a shadow.

I burst through the doors to my chambers, ready to make the blonde suffer for... For... For what exactly? For freeing Farah? For outsmarting me? For making me believe there was a real connection?

The sight of my empty dishevelled bed turned the anger into rage. Fire rampaged through my veins, leaving me trembling in fury. Jade hadn't just stolen a dismembered, broken servant from me, she corrupted someone else, someone that had access to my quarters. Someone that broke into the privacy of my chambers and freed her from her chains. An accomplice. A traitor. A dead man walking.

But who would've dared to enter my chambers and why didn't Jamila catch them? Who dared leave a note on my pillow with instructions to where to find my little maimed puppy? It was obvious I'd have to go to the Summer Resort and deal with Jade there, but then I'd go and unleash my wrath on this poor soul. Who could it be? Who would've known Jade was in here and managed to sneak past Jamila?

The cogs turned in my head and dread sunk in. Jamila... She wouldn't dare... Not after the punishment she received last time. But knowing that nobody else could've accomplished this feat, it had to be her. That little bitch. That insubordinate, traitorous, little bitch.

When I got my hands on her, she'd regret the day she decided to cross me. I would make her and her family suffer until they wished they'd never been born.

Enraged, I stormed out of my chambers and grabbed the first maid I could find.

"You!" I barked, no longer caring about my manners. This was rapidly turning into a disaster.

"Yes, Your Royal Hi—"

"Save it. Find Halim and tell him to wait outside of my chambers. Now!"

"Halim?"

"The palace master's son. Hurry!"

"Yes, Your Royal Highness. At once, Your Royal Highness." Without waiting for her to stop bowing, I raced as fast as my dignity allowed to the Summer Resort. Jade had been fun to play with, but this had gone too far.

The night hid me from any wandering eyes as I crossed the gardens. I didn't know where Franz or any of their servants were, but I imagined if Jade was keeping a mangled woman in there, she'd have found some privacy. But where could she be...

Ah, the balcony. It was attached to a very big room that didn't have a lot of windows. With two emergency doors that were exit only, that was the perfect place for shelter. Perfect.

I glanced behind me, making sure I wasn't followed. With Jamila's betrayal, I'd just have to assume everyone was compromised until I got to the bottom of this. The crickets chirped softly as I left the darkness behind and entered one of the hidden entrances. The stairs swirled up to the balcony Jade and I met on before and I was greeted before I could even stop out of the shadows.

"Princess Zafira. Thank you for joining me."

Chapter 15. Birdy

JADE'S SILKY VOICE greeted me the moment I set foot over the threshold. Five dim candles danced their light into the otherwise dark room. Despite my anger, I couldn't deny how beautiful she looked. This wasn't the same woman I had trembling and quivering under me, no, this was someone entirely else. And as much as she enraged me, this Jade excited me even more than I deemed possible before her.

"I see you had a little birdy to help you," I smiled, masking any emotions that would betray how angered I was.

"Like I said, your handmaiden's help is appreciated."

I knew it. "I'm glad she could be of her service. Where is she?" I asked casually, making note to deal with her after I dealt with Jade.

"Your handmaiden? Oh, she is right here." The blonde smiled deviously and pulled one of the cupboards open. A bound figure tumbled out and I recognised the desperate eyes of Jamila. Her gag prevented her from screaming, but it was clear from her expression that she was distressed. Served her right.

"Do you make it a habit to bind your servants?" I smiled politely, not really understanding why she bound Jamila if she helped her.

"Do you?" Jade countered, throwing a packet at my feet. The towel fell open and a severed hand pointed at me.

"I see you met Farah." I shrugged, making sure to keep my mask impenetrable. So Jade really did get a hold of Farah. I just needed to find out where that woman was so I could silence her forever. I shouldn't have left Halim to deal with her, the incompetent bastard.

"I did, yes. She had lots of interesting things to tell. Very eager to betray her former master." Jade shook her head, scoffing disappointedly. "Not a good quality for a servant. Not at all."

"Very distasteful," I agreed.

"I took the liberty of dealing with her for you," Jade smiled. Another packet thudded at my feet and a second hand and tongue fell on the floor.

"How do I know this is my disobedient servant?" I asked, not putting it past Jade. She could've cut off someone else's limbs for dramatic effect.

"You're thorough," the blonde sighed, beckoning me to join her at the window. Careful not to get blood on my dress, I stepped over the body parts and followed her line of sight.

There was a saying the night could hide a multitude of sins and for the most part, that was true. But not this one. The moon cast a reflection on a new scarecrow in the golden fields. The gentle summer breeze played with the hairs of Farah's severed head and I smiled.

"Does that satisfy you?" Jade stared deeply in my eyes, her green gems capturing my attention.

"Greatly," I replied, ignoring the muffled noises of Jamila on the background.

"I aim to please." She trailed her fingers along my temple in a tender gesture. "Maybe one day you'll let me show you."

"I wouldn't count on it," I whispered back, the scent of orchids luring me towards her.

"That's disappointing."

"I don't sleep with traitors."

Jade broke our gaze, releasing me from her spell. She chuckled to herself and poured two cups of wine. "Drink?"

I stared at her, wondering if she was trying to poison me or test me. Maybe she was daring me to chicken out? But life was meant to be filled with danger and I lived by that rule.

If she wanted me dead, she could've done that before showing me all this. No, she wanted to play the same twisted game I loved and this was no time to back out. I was calling her bluff.

"I'd love to." The glass felt cold in my hand and I made sure to have a subtle sniff before I brought it to my lips. Because of our religion, alcohol wasn't a common beverage, but the royal family liked to indulge. "Salud."

The cold liquid rolled over my tongue and I knew I was playing with fire. The moment I swallowed this sip, I could've sealed my own fate. The uncertainty of the moment, the risk I was taking, it was exhilarating. Raw adrenaline danced through my veins as I swallowed the wine. To die or not to die.

"Not afraid it was poisoned?" Jade arched an eyebrow and stared at me daringly. I hid a smile, so I'd been right. She did want to make me think of poison. But if she was trying to scare me, it wasn't working. I wasn't afraid, no I was excited.

"No, I'm not." I stared into her dark eyes, watching her swivel the wine in her glass.

She chuckled softly and took a swig from her own cup. "Salud."

Pleased that I got it right, I took another sip of the wine. Hints of cherry and red fruit danced on my palate and I imagined they'd go great with a taste of Jade.

The muffled cries of Jamila broke the intimate moment and I sighed. "Why is she bound?"

"I have no use for her anymore. And I wouldn't want her to run off."

"Do your servants often run off?"

Jade pushed her beautiful hair behind her ear, mischief painted on her face. "Mine don't, but I don't know about yours."

Mine? I stared at the two women and let the cogs turn in my head. If Jade didn't consider Jamila her pawn, maybe my handmaiden hadn't betrayed me on purpose. Maybe Jade threatened her, but with what? There was only one thing Jamila loved more than me and that was her family.

Ah damn.

"Her sister is such a lovely child. Isn't that what I said, Jamila?" Jade patted the crying woman's cheek and laughed harshly. "I told her I'd have her little sister beheaded if she didn't unchain and escort me to the Summer Resort. I think it's fairly obvious what she chose."

"I see." I studied the distraught features of my handmaiden. What a shame. She served me well over the years.

"So not loyal to me... Not loyal to you," Jade hummed, boring her heel into Jamila's hand. "I wonder what we should do with her."

"Do with her what you want, I have no longer any use of her." Even if she hadn't conspired against me, her act of selfishness counted as high treason. I had no need for a handmaiden that feared an empty threat more than me.

"Let's see what she has to say about the matter."

The moment she tugged the gag down, Jamila cried out to me.

"Please, Your Royal Highness, I didn't mean to betray you. Please, she threatened my family, my baby sister. I didn't think—"

"She annoys me. Gag her again," I yawned, not interested in her pleas. Jamila's eyes shone with despair as Jade pushed the cloth back in her mouth. Her tears stained the stone floor and yet, I didn't feel any empathy for her. I didn't know what that meant.

"Not attached to your handmaiden? The one that served you for many years?" The woman opposite of me took another sip of her wine and painted an alluring smile on her lips. "Jamila has been by your side for so long, don't you feel any compassion towards her ordeal?"

"I have other handmaidens," I shrugged, staring at the blonde. What was she trying to achieve by threatening Jamila? I didn't care.

But maybe Jade didn't know that yet. Maybe she was trying to gauge just how twisted I was.

Oh, that was interesting. I hadn't considered that. Why hadn't I? I assumed Jade was made out of the same cloth as I, so why hadn't I assumed she was doing the same thing? Trying to figure out just how twisted her opponent was.

This was a test. But what was she testing?

"So you wouldn't care if I disposed of her for you?"

Jamila cried into her gag, crawling pathetically over the floor to me. Did she think I was going to save her?

Oh, that was it. Jade wanted to know how attached I got to people by killing her in front of my eyes. How deviously clever of her. Did she really think I was going to reveal my twisted nature to her?

But then again, this was my chance to discover hers. Would she really do it? Kill someone with her own hands? Squeeze the life out of a breathing woman, feel a beating heart grow still? Would she be able to do it without batting an eye?

Did I want to gamble exposing my true self for the exposure of hers?

Yes, yes I did.

She wouldn't be around for long, I would make sure of that. But for once, I wanted to know what it was to feel connected to someone. Other people kept going on and on about it. Friends, family, lovers. That inherent kinship humans felt and I lacked. Maybe, just once, I wouldn't be alone.

"I have no attachment to this woman," I smiled, ignoring Jamila's desperate cries. I'd just find myself a new handmaiden, choice enough.

"If you say so," Jade sang, pulling a knife from out of her dress. Where she kept that, was a mystery. I definitely hadn't felt it when I undressed her. "Let's give her a chance to beg for her life, shall we?"

She tore the gag off and Jamila fell to my feet. "I beg you, help me. Your Royal Highness. I'm so sorry I disobeyed you, I won't ever do it again. I promise, never, never. Please, help me."

"But you did. You let Princess Jade leave and I was nowhere near done with her," I said, catching the blonde's gaze. There was a darkness I recognised, a darkness I adored. I'd been right from the very start. She wasn't an good person, not at all. But how twisted was she really?

I was about to find out.

Chapter 16. Family

"YOU SERVED ME WELL, Jamila," I spoke. Her eyes filled with hope and I refrained from laughing. People were pathetic. "But this is the end. Thank you for your service."

"No! No, please, no! I need to take care of my family. My little sister, she's only five. She needs the money for her school, please, Your Highness. I beg of you, forgive me, I will serve you my whole life, I'll do anything you want. Anything."

I crouched down next to her and touched her cheek. "Don't you see... You *have* served me your whole life." I brushed a tear away, studying the anguish in her eyes. She didn't seem too concerned about her own life, instead, she kept blabbering about her family. Was this love?

"I beg you, please, Your Royal Highness. *Zafira.* Please!" she sobbed, my name rolling off her tongue for the first time ever. How impudent, yet interesting.

"You'll do anything for your family?" I asked, curious about her reaction. She wasn't the first who begged, not at all. But it felt different... She wasn't giving up, not even when I made it crystal clear I wasn't going to save her. Why? What kept her going on? Why didn't she accept her fate?

"Anything, I promise. Anything. I just want my family to be safe, for my little sister to grow up better than I did."

I shot Jade a look, asking her for a moment. The blonde studied me, her eyes boring deeply into mine. Was she reading my blackened soul?

She didn't interfere, so I took that as a good sign. I brushed a strand of hair behind Jamila's ear and smiled. "With one word to the palace master, he'll send more riches to your family than they've ever seen. They'd have enough for their whole lives and so would your sister. But for that to happen, I need you to do one thing for me."

"Yes, please, anything!"

My lips curled up in a devious grin. Perfect. "I need you to die."

From the corner, I heard Jade's surprised cough, but I dismissed it. This was far too fascinating.

"What?" Jamila stared at me hesitantly.

"I need you to die," I repeated myself, not sure why she was confused. My request was very simple.

"But..."

"Looks like your family is starving then." I turned away from her and brushed the dust off my dress.

"Wait!"

Ah, music to my ears. "I'm listening."

"If I die, you swear you'll take care of my family?"

"You have my word."

My handmaiden stared at me, her eyes swimming with tears. She looked at Jade, probably wondering how serious she was. That made two of us. I was calling her bluff, but would she actually do it?

"What's your final answer?" I stared at Jamila's expression and found the answer before she even opened her mouth.

"Yes. I'll do it."

I studied the exchange in her eyes and found something new, something different. Like all the other women, the life was leaking out of her before she actually met her death. Unlike the others, she wasn't panicked or desperate. She looked resolved, almost... at peace?

Interesting, but not nearly as fascinating or exciting as despair. It already bored me. I waved at Jade and shrugged. "I'm done with her."

"I see." She twirled the knife between her fingers and sighed as she placed the blade against Jamila's throat. "You feel no attachment to your loyal servant?"

"No, I don't." I caught her green eyes and smiled. Showtime. Bluff or no bluff.

"There's no going back after this."

"I don't do regret."

The first drop of blood trickled out of the shallow cut. Jamila whimpered but didn't protest. I read the fear on her face, but the determination in her eyes didn't waver. She really was going to sacrifice herself for her family.

"Last chance to stop me," Jade breathed. I felt the tension curl around my chest as I was about to witness something glorious, something unique. The scent of flowers made the strenuous moment all the more beautiful and licked my lips.

I stared the blonde in her green eyes, my mask slipping to reveal my true nature. Moment of truth. "Go ahead."

I dare you.

Chapter 17. Poison

THE LIGHT OF THE CANDLES reflected in the blade as Jade waved it in front of Jamila's eyes. She chuckled as she hid the knife under her dress again. "Far too messy," she explained, walking her fingers over the table. "But it silences chatty people."

I nodded, well aware of how tedious it was to clean up blood. Even after Halim's scrubbing, I noticed blood residue in the dungeons. Having the Summer Resort cleaned would probably arouse some suspicion and I didn't feel like being under scrutiny when I tried disposing of a princess.

Jade picked up an old pillowcase from the closet and nodded to herself. "This'll do. Any last words?" she asked, but I wasn't sure if she meant me or my handmaiden. Instead of gracing her with a reply, I caught Jamila's gaze and waited for the realisation to sink in. There was no way somebody was this quiet and resolved about their death.

The blonde curled the dusty rag around Jamila's throat and slowly twisted the fabric tighter and tighter until her reflexes kicked in. Even if she wanted to embrace death, her body wouldn't let that happen. Not without a fight. She gasped for air, clawing at the constraint.

"Shhh, shh, it'll be over soon," Jade whispered. The noose suffocated the life out of Jamila and with every passing second, she grew more desperate to escape. I sighed as I witnessed her struggle. Not different from other people after all then. Boring.

Instead of watching my handmaiden, I darted my eyes up to the blonde. Huh. Now that was different. Excitement was dancing across her features, but it wasn't about Jamila's death. She wasn't even looking at her. No, it was about me. She was elated about me.

My handmaiden grew still as she fell into a deep slumber she wouldn't ever wake up from and thudded to the ground. As Jade stepped over the lifeless body, I figured out what the smile on her face was about. A thrill ran down my spine as I came to the same conclusion as her. A wicked grin spread across Jade's face and I knew I was mimicking it.

She was like me, *exactly* like me. Maybe I'd keep her around for just a moment longer and enjoy the twisted games we could play.

"Zafira, Zafira, Zafira... You surprise me." Jade arched her eyebrow, an amused look gracing her face.

"No, I don't."

"Oh, yes you do. Who would've thought,"

"Who would've thought what?" I asked sweetly, stepping over Jamila's body. Jade's body radiated off heat and the memory of her touch had me wanting more.

"The beautiful flower of the East, Zafira Zahran Al Abbassi. Esteemed princess, beloved daughter, adored sister... Rotten to the core."

I chuckled throatily, shaking my head in amusement. "I hold no candle to the radiant gem of the West, Jade Sophia of Liechtenstein. With your captivating green eyes and enchanting way of words, none would've guessed you were dark as the devil."

"You flatter me," she grinned. Her hand found my waist and I fell into her, drawn in by the alluring scent of orchids and the promise of something much sweeter. Her lips brushed over mine, gently, tenderly. A little lie between the two of us, like a secret. There was nothing remotely sweet or kind about the two of us.

"I'm afraid I might have to call upon your help once more, Princess Jade," I breathed as I feathered butterfly kisses along her jaw.

"Your wish is my command, Your Royal Highness." She nipped at my earlobe and chuckled breathily as the goosebumps ran up my skin. "Where to next?"

"My chambers. I've got someone waiting for me."

If that threw her off, it didn't show. "Lead the way."

"Make sure to bring that knife of yours," I hinted, catching a glimmer in her eyes. So she liked that?

"I've got it right here." She took my hand and guided it into her dress. My fingers brushed past endless soft skin until they bumped into the cold steel. I took the opportunity to stroke her side and press another kiss on her lips.

"Perfect. We'll need it."

The night concealed the two of us and our well-kept secret. There was something oddly comforting about having Jade with me. Maybe it was the relief of not having to hide all my deepest and darkest desires around her. Or the pleasure of knowing exactly what to expect from her.

Our footsteps echoed into the corridors as we rushed to my private quarters. Without Jamila, there was nobody guarding the hidden entrance behind the eagle statue. Inside of my chambers, I pulled open a secret compartment and revealed a jug of wine. I made sure to conceal the crystal glasses as I poured the alcohol into them. With an innocent smile, I presented her with a glass.

"Drink?" I asked, turning the tables. Now that she knew exactly what I was, would she call my bluff and dare drink the wine?

"I'd love to." She curled her hand around the glass and tipped it towards her lips. With a never-wavering smile, she took a sip and stared confidently at me. She clearly didn't have any problem gambling either. How exciting. I waited just an extra moment until I brought the wine to my lips and had a taste of my own. I could've poisoned her but that wasn't a very creative way to get rid off her. I'd take care of her later, after I had my fun. I deserved some proper play time.

"Would you excuse me for a moment?" I asked, enjoying the formal and informal banter we had going on. There was something utterly ironic about being all proper just after disposing of two people. If Halim was waiting for me as expected, maybe we could make that three. Although after his mistake, he deserved a punishment befitting that crime. Death was too easy and short-lived. I needed something better, something that would haunt him for life without it putting me in danger of him exposing our dungeon activities. Although with me being the princess, there really wasn't any chance of Father believing him over me, but I didn't need that kind of suspicion around me.

I swung the main doors open into the welcome hall. No Halim. That was a bit concerning. Did that stupid servant not find him or did he choose not to come?

What was happening... Ever since Jade entered my life, I seemed to be losing control over... Over everything.

I crossed the hall into the public corridor and found my two guards, both to protect and contain me. I nodded at Azim, not too bothered for having him at my door. I'd known him for so long, I'd watched his hair turn grey and his wrinkles grow deeper. Between him and the angry Jalal who only got here a couple of years ago, I knew who I preferred. Everytime he looked at me, I detected a glint of something perverse in his eyes, a strange kind of lust. Not exactly the kind of guard I'd want, but Father insisted on having him there. Didn't mean I had to acknowledge him.

"Masaa' al-khayr, Azim." I gave him a fake smile as I wished him a good evening.

"Masaa'an-nuur, Your Royal Highness. What can I do for you today?"

"Any unusual activity today?" I gave that servant an order, but she wasn't waiting for me in the welcome hall. Wasn't she trained properly?

"No, nothing out of the ordinary."

"Thank you." With a calm and collected demeanour, I wished him a good night and pulled the doors shut. The moment the locks clicked shut, I allowed the rage to bubble up.

"Aaargh!" I slammed the porcelain vase on the ground and watched it shatter in a thousand pieces. Every sliver reflected my own enraged face into the shiny finish and I studied myself. When did I become this temperamental? What happened that my emotions were getting the better of me? Why didn't I feel in control anymore? What changed?

I scoffed, glaring at my private chambers. I knew exactly what changed. There was a devious blonde sitting on my bed that had me running around her in circles with no regard for anything else.

I couldn't even remember the last time I thought about overthrowing my brother, no I'd been too focussed on Jade and all her games to think about the Crown. And in return, it had cost me two servants.

She needed to go. Tonight.

Resolved, I took in a deep breath and buried all the frustration. I straightened out my dress and marched back to my chambers. No matter the consequences, I needed to get rid of the princess once and for all. Having her around was too big of a threat and I couldn't have that kind of distraction, not when I was aiming to be Queen.

I'd have to get my own hands dirty this time, unfortunately. Not exactly something to look forward to, but what had to happen had to happen. I just needed to figure out the right method. Poison would be too straight forward and would never hold up as an accident. A quick slit to the throat sounded good in theory, but far too messy and too slow. Unlike theatrical portrayal, it was agonisingly time-consuming and a pain to clean up. Not something I'd want in my own chambers.

Suffocation? Jade seemed quite strong. Holding her down would prove to be quite challenging, but not impossible.

Huh. I didn't actually know how to kill someone, not without arousing suspicion and have neon lights pointing at me. How... utterly disgraceful. Up till this point, I'd used my power over people to get what I wanted. As the princess, they were in no position to protest or even think about making their countermove. But Jade... No, she had her own twisted ways and the power to have the plebs of the world do her bidding. She demonstrated that earlier by using one of my pawns for her own gain. Quite clever, really. But if she thought she was getting the upper hand, she was wrong. Now it was my move in a power play of wits, manipulation, and true darkness. *Game on.*

Until I got to know Jade better, I wouldn't be able to dispose of her. Not without putting my own noose around my neck. No, I needed to play along, for now. Let her believe she was in control of the situation, of the palace, of me.

I'd keep her around until I could create the perfect opportunity. It was too much of a risk to just kill her. That was the only reason I was keeping her alive. It was. Why else would I let someone off the hook?

No, Zafira. She isn't off the hook. I was just extending her stay so I had more time to figure out how to make her life a living hell. All I needed was a little bit of extra time. That was for tomorrow. Tonight, I would allow myself something rare, something special. A little treat.

With that thought in mind, I pushed the bedroom door open to a crack and found myself in the dim orange glow of a single candle. A shadow brushed past me and two soft hands covered up my eyes. Jade's warm breath tickled the shell of my ear as she pressed herself against my back. "If this was anyone else, wouldn't it almost be romantic?" she whispered, the amusement clear in her voice.

"Depends on what you believe romance is," I grinned back, letting her guide me forward.

"Maybe this is." A soft kiss fell on the back of my neck, so tender it could've been mistaken for a real kiss.

"Your idea of romance is kissing someone with a knife strapped against your thigh?" I teased, tapping her upper leg where I felt the steel pressing into my skin.

"Call it a precaution for the next time you decide to chain me to your bed."

"So you're hoping there will be a next time?" Instead of taking another step forward, I paused so she bumped into me. Her warm body curved against mine and I shivered. Regardless of who she was, or what she was, I couldn't deny she drew me in like a moth to a flame. And the risk of getting burned was a real threat. A real promise.

"Depends... Can you guarantee you won't do it again?" Jade curled her arm around me as my knees hit the edge of the bed. Her lips found my neck again and another butterfly kiss tickled my skin.

A grin lifted my face and I shook my head. "No promises."

"That's what I thought." She reached past me and pushed the shackles away. "But you won't need them tonight. I have no intention of leaving." Abruptly, she shoved me down on the bed and tangled her hands in my hair. At the same time as she pushed her hand between my legs, her teeth scraped over my skin. Every inch of me wanted to protest, but all I did was shiver under her touch. Her growl left me with goosebumps and her soft moan brought life to something else, something not many people could awaken. Something not many *wanted* to unleash. There was no use in pretending anymore. No, we finally put our cards on the table. But that didn't mean ended. Not with the aces I had up my sleeve.

Excitement flooded my body with a thrill I hadn't had in a long time. Her hand curved up and I moaned as she slipped her fingers inside of me. "This time, I'm in control."

Without time to protest, she found the sensitive bundle of nerves hidden between my folds and the words fell out of my head. There was something primal, something animalistic about the way she was touching me. The heat from her kisses on my shoulder, her curled up demanding fingers, her encouraging whispers edging me on. If I'd be able to, I'd have flipped myself around, but the pleasure coursing through me stole my control. Everything about this was utterly shameful. The vulnerable position, Jade's dirty suggestions in my ear, and the undeniable pleasure building inside of me. Disgraceful.

I loved it.

I wished my body was lying, that I was just reacting to her touch to trick her into believing she could play me like a fiddle. But the circles she rubbed were excruciatingly slow, the spots she touched far too sensitive, far too secret, far too pleasurable. Right now, I would be embracing the submissive role, just for the night. Just until she tipped me over the edge and had me trembling uncontrollably.

Yes, I'd make her pay for this, although I wasn't entirely sure what 'this' was. The way she had a hold over me? How she was giving me unearthly pleasures? For making me enjoy being on the bottom?

It was all a bit vague in my mind. The haze was setting in and my brain was running the same circles Jade was rubbing. One by one, thoughts fell out of my head. Thoughts of revenge, thoughts of revolution, thoughts of taking the Crown, thoughts of disposing of Jade, thoughts of controlling the world. With every little flick of her thumb, every curled up finger sliding over my sensitive spot, every trail her nails left on my back, my mind stopped stringing words together. Her touches become more insistent, harder, rougher. Demanding. I arched into her, no longer caring about how I was appearing, about what she was thinking. I was close and I wanted it.

"Not so in control now, are we?" Jade grinned, biting into my shoulder. The sharp sting added to the heat coursing through me and shot straight to my core.

"Shut up and do me," I panted, sounding frustratedly needy instead of powerful.

"Ask me nicely," she chuckled, her nails drawing lines into my back. The infuriating pain heightened my senses and I bucked against her. If she thought I was asking her, she had another thing coming.

"I swear, if you're going to be a bitch, I will bring out the shackles," I barked, my authority lost in the moans of ecstasy as she quickened her pace. The gentle ripples turned into insistent waves threatening to wash over me. It almost wasn't bearable anymore. "Don't you dare—"

The blonde coiled her hand up, hitting all the right spots at once and chuckled throatily. "I have no intention of stopping. Not if you ask me nicely."

"Fuck you."

"I didn't hear a question."

Damn her. She really wanted me to say it and with every circle, every flick, every insufferably sexy moan, my resistance lessened.

"I'm listening, Princess."

My hands balled into fists as I gripped the sheets, my knuckles turning white in frustration. I wanted to and I hated that I wanted to. I didn't want her to stop, I wanted the release, the pleasure, the satisfaction only she could bring.

"Please, make me." The very moment my plea rolled off my tongue, she shoved three fingers inside of me and hit the exact spot that turned the world off. The waves finally crashed over me and it felt even better than I hoped it to be. I screamed curses into the bedding when she tipped me over the edge, leaving me defenseless and powerless under her mercy. White spots danced in front of my eyes as she stole my control and had me trembling pathetically on her fingers.

I hated her. I hated her for making me feel this good, for robbing me of the power I shrouded myself in my entire life, for making me quiver under her touch. I hated her for this, for all of this. But mostly, I hated myself for loving it.

"You're beautiful when you beg," Jade smirked, wiping her hand on my sheets. I'd scold her for it when I finally found my voice again. Instead, I turned on the bed and slapped her thigh. She deserved that. Pathetic, but that was the best I had.

"That's not a nice way of thanking me."

"Oh, you'll know when I'm thanking you," I spat back, humiliated for the whimpering mess she turned me into. How dared she make me beg.

I rearranged my dress, embarrassed she hadn't even taken off my clothes. Like doing a slut in a backway alley. If she wasn't a princess, I'd have her beheaded on the spot. But I couldn't do that, not without getting in all sorts of trouble. But that didn't mean I would just let this happen. No, my revenge would be sweet and everything she didn't see coming.

"I'm waiting," Jade sang.

"Get out," I commanded, finally back in control of my traitorous emotions.

"As you wish, Your Royal Highness," she mocked, bowing deeply and picking up her cardigan. Whistling, she strolled out of the room. Just as she pulled the door shut, she shot me another look. "Goodnight, Zafira."

"Out!"

The door slammed in its lock and I fell back on the bed. The whirlwind finally settled down and returned me to my regular self. That Jade was infuriating and as I replayed the events of the night in my head, I found my hand pushing my dress open again. As much as I hated to admit it, she definitely hit the right spot. The vulnerable position she forced me into was repulsive, revolting, appallingly submissive. I shouldn't have enjoyed it and yet there was no denying that I did.

How twisted, how backwards, how wrong. How sexy.

Chapter 18. Orange blossoms

THE MORNING BROKE THROUGH the windows and I uncurled from my sheets. The new day brought new opportunities and I was ready to be reborn. Last night, Jade jerked me around like a fool. Today, she was going to die. I'd make sure of it.

"Jami—" I shouted, only halfway through remembering the fate of my handmaiden. Ah, that was annoying. I should make sure to get a new servant assigned to that task. I'd get to that first thing. Killing Jade could be next on my list.

I browsed through the vast array of clothes I had and picked a summery dress. It seemed quite a celebratory choice and would fit the joyous occasion of bringing Jade's end. She well deserved that after the stunt she pulled last night.

The early sun brushed my skin as I quickly passed the patio and joined the great hall to greet my parents. As always, Mother glared as I entered, the jealousy unmistakable in her eyes. She detested the fact I was a younger, more beautiful version of her. On the other hand, Father's face lit up as he welcomed me.

"Sabah al-khyr, my child."

"Morning, Father." I ignored Jade and Franz in the guest section and took my place next to his throne. A handful of my servants joined me hesitantly, clearly confused without Jamila's direction. I pointed at one of them and beckoned her closer. The excitement danced across her face as she bowed at my feet.

"Your Royal Highness, how can I serve you today?"

"Call the palace master."

"Of course, Your Royal Highness. At once, Your Royal Highness."

I caught her wrist before she left. "One 'Your Royal Highness' is enough."

"Certainly, Your Royal Highness."

"Are you new?"

The young woman coloured red, her blushes answering my question. "I'm on a trial period, Your Royal Highness."

"What's your name?"

"Leah, Your Royal Highness."

I nodded, giving her a smile. "Perfect. Now get the palace master."

The young woman scrambled away, racing to the old man at Father's side. I heard all the other servants murmur and gossip as they all knew she was being too ungraceful and clunky. But I quite liked her eagerness to please. That was always a good quality, especially now that I was looking for a new handmaiden.

From behind my fan, I stole a glance at the blonde across the room and caught her eyes. Jade licked her lips seductively and gave me a secret wink. The nerve.

I clicked my tongue very unladylike and averted my gaze. I wouldn't grace her with my attention until I came up with a way of putting her back in her place. At this rate, I was failing miserably at regaining the high ground. I needed to figure something out and quick. What if she lost interest?

Oh fuck. No, that wasn't what I meant. No, I didn't care if she lost interest. No, I needed to get back to her to punish her for her... For her... Disobedience. That was why. I scoffed under my breath and picked at the tangerine in front of me. I wasn't exactly hungry.

The palace master approached my seat and bowed deeply. More bootlicking. Great.

"What can I do for you, Your Royal Highness Zafira?"

"I'm in need for a new handmaiden. Set it up."

"Don't you have Jamila in your service?"

I gave him a disapproving glare and waited. It was none of his business what happened to my servants. Not if I didn't want it to be.

He wavered for a moment and bowed deeply again. "My apologies, Your Royal Highness Zafira, it's none of my business. I'll set up the selection."

I dismissed him with a little wave of my hand and he quickly weaseled away. How that wet towel got a son like Halim was a real mystery. I nibbled on the tangerine and decided I'd do without a breakfast today. The lukewarm water was pleasant on my skin as I dipped my hands in for a rinse. Despite Jamila not being here, the usual little orange blossoms were floating in them. Impressive.

"Who put those flowers in there?" I asked, staring at the group of nameless servants. They all whispered and looked at each other, clearly not sure whether I was about to reward or punish someone. It took a bit of shuffling before the same young woman as before was pushed forward.

"I picked and washed them, Your Royal Highness."

"Leah, correct?"

"Yes, Your Royal Highness."

I nodded, not displeased with this new servant. "Very nice."

She fell to her knees and kissed my feet. "You honour me, Your Royal Highness. Thank you, Your Royal Highness."

"Leah?"

"Yes, Your Royal Highness?"

"Once is enough."

"Of course, my sincere apologies. I won't forget!" she hurried back to her place, almost tripping over her robe. Just as she sat down, she remembered something and fell back to her knees. "Your Royal Highness!"

I rose to my feet and bowed to Father. "May I be excused, Father?"

"You may, my child."

I ignored Mother's annoyed glare and purposefully didn't look at Jade either. With my head held high, I marched out of the hall and enjoyed the two seconds of solitude until the horde of servants caught on. They squabled over who'd carry the shade as I waited in the sun. If they didn't hurry, I'd blister. Damn, I really needed a new handmaiden.

Inside the patio, I made my way to the stands and sat down at the top seat. The palace master was still shouting orders at random women and lining them up. Lots of candidates. That was a good sign. He pointed at the rest of my servants and chased them into the middle. The flock of women scrambled and dispersed into the crowd.

"Mind if I join you, Your Royal Highness?" A male voice asked for my attention and I found Franz standing at the foot of the tribune.

"Be welcome," I smiled, inviting him up. Maybe he could give me some intel on his sister and get me a leg up on how to make her life sour.

"Picking a new handmaiden?"

"As one must do every now and then." I didn't want to encourage him to spend more time with me, so I whipped out my stiffest words. If I bored him, hopefully he'd leave me alone.

"Back at the palace, I used to help my sister with the selection. It'd be my honour if I could be of your assistance."

"Your assistance would be most appreciated," I lied, only putting up with him for his sister. How one could be so alluring and the other so bland was particularly curious. But of course, I couldn't show any of my dislike for him. At least it wasn't personal. I Just didn't like anyone. Apart from Jade.

Damn it, no I didn't like Jade! That was an atrocious thought. I shook it out of my head and focussed to the task on hand. Picking a new handmaiden, one that hopefully didn't end with her strangled in the Summer Resort.

The palace master bowed and cleared his throat. "When you're ready, Your Royal Highness Zafira."

I waved him away and studied the group of women in front of me. Most of them were quite unmemorable, just how I liked it. I didn't want anyone that would outshine me. "Number four."

The middle-aged woman was ushered to me and bowed deeply.

"Name?"

"Nadiya, Your Royal Highness Zafira."

"Tell me something about yourself."

The woman cleared her throat. "I was born in a little village not far from here, I have three sisters and—"

"Thank you. Next," I dismissed her, already bored. I didn't need to know these kind of things and if she thought I cared, she wouldn't be a good fit for my servants. "Number thirteen."

The palace master snapped his fingers and the young woman skipped to the front. She dipped through her knees like a little schoolgirl and I refrained from rolling my eyes. "No, next."

"If I may?" Franz said, disturbing my thoughts. Another repressed eye roll later, I smiled at him and nodded politely.

"I'd be honoured."

"That one there, number seven."

I nodded at the palace master. "Approach."

The older woman marched towards me, quite heavy on her feet. It reminded me of an elephant stomping around and not exactly what I wanted in the morning. That was why I hadn't picked number seven, but to humour our guest, I pretended it was a good choice.

"Name?"

"Sanaa, ready to serve you, Your Royal Highness Zafira."

"Tell me a little about yourself."

"I keep a tight house. Cleaning, cooking, ironing, I can do it all, Your Royal Highness Zafira."

"Lovely." I didn't need a maid, we had servants for that already. So much for Franz's good taste. "Next. There, fifteen."

The next candidate ran to the front and bowed, swishing her dress as she did. Dramatic. "No, next. There, number two."

Another young woman quickly scurried to my side and bowed until her nose touched the dust. "At your service, Your Royal Highness Zafira."

"Name?"

"Nima, Your Royal Highness Zafira."

"Tell me about yourself."

"I'm quick on my feet, I don't have a lot of experience but I'm very willing to learn. Eager. I'm here to please you and fulfil all your wishes. Your Royal Highness Zafira."

"Continue."

"I'm ready to commit to your service, day and night, whatever you desire, I will get it done."

"Very promising. Next." I stared at the young woman from earlier and nodded at her. "Number seventeen."

She rushed towards me, tripping over the hem of her dress in her hurry to get to me. She bowed clumsily, far deeper than needed. She really was too clumsy, but there was something about her, something endearing. Like a little puppy.

"Name?"

"Your Royal Highness Zafira, no, sorry, my name is not Zafira, I meant to say my name was Leah. I didn't mean Zafira, that's you. Not just Zafira, oh no, I meant Your Royal Hi—"

I held up one finger, hoping to silence her rambling. She took a moment to regain her composure and took a deep breath.

"My name is Leah, Your Royal Highness."

"Tell me more about yourself."

"What would you like to know, Your Royal Highness?"

I hid a smile. "Who taught you your manners?"

"My aunt, Your Royal Highness. She had a good tuition and taught me everything I know." She made another bow, clearly not used to the palace life. She was new, inexperienced, perfect to mould in whatever I wanted. So innocent and gullible, the perfect blank slate. Easy to corrupt, to taint, to shape.

I really was a monster... In an uncharacteristic moment, I decided it would be better if I kept this young woman as far from my claws as possible.

"We're done here." I waved the palace master over. "Send them my thanks and then send them home."

"Of course, Your Royal Highness. At once. Have you made a decision?

"May I?" Franz asked, holding out his hand to help me off the tribune. I placed my palm on his and pretended I needed someone to guide me down. As if I couldn't do that by myself. Men. "I heard the gardens are particularly beautiful at this time of the year. I would love if you could accompany me."

"That sounds delightful, but I'm afraid the sun isn't treating me well," I smiled, declining his offer graciously but firmly. I didn't have time for this, I was in the middle of my war with Jade.

"Your Highness, I'm afraid I can't take no for an answer."

"*Prince* Franz, if you need a tour of the gardens, I invite you to talk to the palace master."

He grabbed my wrist and yanked me to him. "And I invite you to grant me this request, Princess."

I snapped my hand back and growled lowly. "I could have you beheaded for this."

"I am well aware of that fact, so you must realise how desperate I am."

"I sympathise." Lie. "But I have nothing to do with your desperation." Ready to walk away, I turned on my heels. Maybe I should get him executed for this, that should rattle his sister.

"You have everything to do with my desperation. She was in your bed last night."

I froze, shaken by his knowledge. How did he know and why didn't I know he knew? Without giving away anything, I refaced him with my politest smile. "Continue."

"Not here. The gardens, half an hour, no servants."

"That's not a very proper proposition."

"I'm not a very proper man." He strode away, leaving me staring at his back. What was with these siblings? If he wanted to meet me, maybe I'd bring the guillotine with me. That would serve him right for touching me without my permission. But then if I'd be able to learn a bit more about Jade, maybe it was worth listening to him first and then have him punished. But for that, I needed a handmaiden.

I turned to the leaving group of chattering women and snapped my fingers. I shouldn't be doing that, but I was getting sick of all the charades. "You. Report to the palace master as my new handmaiden."

The young woman pointed at herself. "Me, Your Royal Highness?"

"Yes, you. Meet me in the gardens in forty-five minutes with two guards. Don't leave me waiting."

Leah nodded, her face lit up with excitement as she ran after the old man. Guessed nobody was saving her then. Oh well. What a shame.

Chapter 19. Handmaiden

THE AFTERNOON SUN BURNED into my skin as I waited for Franz to show up at the gazebo. If he made me wait one more minute, I'd have him flogged and hung out for the birds. He'd make a good addition to the new scarecrow.

"Your Royal Highness Zafira."

I didn't move a muscle. "Your Serene Highness Franz."

"Thank you for joining me."

"You didn't leave me much choice."

He brushed his hand through his blonde hair and cracked a smile. "Absolutely beautiful gardens."

"Why did you want to see me here."

"Right to the point, then?"

"I have other businesses to attend to," I smiled. All the politeness was an absolute pain, but I couldn't lose my temper. In a perfect world, I'd have everyone dancing on strings, but this wasn't a perfect world. Not yet.

"Are we alone?"

"Unless my eyes betray me, we are."

"I need to confide in you, but I need to stress the utmost importance of discretion here."

"My lips are sealed." That was a lie, but he didn't need to know that. Not yet. He'd find out when I used all his information against him.

"Okay." He looked over his shoulder as he ran his hands through his hair again. His whole demeanour changed and the nerves came out. He'd been doing a bad job hiding that twitching eye of his. And the sweat pearling on his forehead. "Okay... Okay, okay, okay," he muttered to himself, wringing his hands skittishly. He paced back and forth in the gazebo, his features twisted in a grimace.

"Your Serene Highness, you can confide in me," I said softly, placing a hand on his forearm. I heard that was a comforting gesture and he was clearly holding onto a dear secret. A secret I wanted to know.

"Okay, but what I'm saying can't leave this gazebo. Not if we want to avoid a political war."

"I'm listening." I leaned in, a little more intrigued now. If this could avoid a war, I was sure it could start one too. And if there was one thing I enjoyed, it was chaos.

"Princess Jade... Or at least, the woman you know as Princess Jade..."

"Yes?" I didn't even have to fake my interest, I wanted to know everything and anything about his mysterious sister.

"She's not my sister."

"Oh my goodness," I gasped, using my fan to hide my open mouth. Now *that* was a real revelation. "Forgive me if I misunderstood, but I don't believe I understand."

"I have a sister, a real sister. She is named Jade, but this woman I brought to your palace... That's not her."

I kept quiet, egging him on to continue. Now I was finally getting to the good stuff.

"This woman, this imposter... She took us by surprise during our travels. Her accomplice is holding the real princess hostage and she's using me to keep up the pretenses."

"Outrageous." So that was how it was. Now that really changed things. Oh, how it changed the complete game. With this new piece of information, it wouldn't be hard to take control back. She wasn't a real princess and so having her executed wouldn't be a problem. "What are her demands?"

"She won't return my sister until she has her hands on the Crown."

"I'm afraid I don't understand what kind of help I could be to you. Are you wanting to call upon our executioner?"

The prince waved his hands, stammering and stuttering. "No, no, heavens, no. If she dies, my sister dies. She made it perfectly clear what would happen if she didn't get what she desired."

"I see..." That made things a little more complicated. I still wanted her gone, but if killing her would kill the real princess, I was back at square one. Unless I made it look like Franz took it upon himself to put an end to her? With the hostage situation, it wouldn't be a stretch of the imagination that he decided he couldn't wait anymore. That would solve a lot of problems. No woman marrying my brother and stealing the throne, no annoying blonde royalty in my palace, and no more Jade. That last one almost seemed sad, but I didn't want to admit that. I couldn't. I had to get rid off her, she was far too dangerous and unpredictable. Having her here could mean serious problems for me. It could even reveal all the hard work I'd been doing for the past years and make all the pretending and lying for nothing.

No, I couldn't let that happen. I wasn't about to let this alluring blonde get in the way of me and *my* Crown. But for that, I needed to get the jump on her first. And maybe this prince could give me an idea of how to do it.

"I'm afraid I'm clueless about how I can be of assistance, Your Serene Highness."

"I need her to believe she's going to marry His Royal Highness Oumar so she'll let my sister go."

"Forgive me for asking, but won't she dispose of your sister when she gets her way?" He shook his head, saddened by this thing that was plaguing him. "I don't know, I don't know. But I can't risk her killing off my sister if she gets rejected. I need you to help make her believe she's getting what she wants."

That was an interesting play. If I actually intended to help him, I was sure it'd be easy enough to have my brother ask for her hand in marriage. I'd seen how he looked at her. But I wouldn't be going along with this madness, no, I'd use this information to get rid of her once and for all.

I fanned myself with cold air. "Naturally, you can understand that I can't allow an imposter to actually wed my brother. Marriage is sacred under His eye."

"Of course, that would be sacrilegious."

"I'll do the best I can, but I'm not well-versed in lying or scheming."

"You're a princess, of course you're well-versed in lying." Franz scoffed as he glared at me. They were truly forward in the West. A man from here would never be allowed to look at me this openly, this bluntly, this vulgarly.

"I'll do my utmost best to ensure a beneficial outcome for the both of us." I smiled politely, hoping he believed that I was playing along.

"Your help is most appreciated, Your Royal Highness Zafira." He bowed deeply, his features relaxing a little. So he did trust I'd keep my word. The fool.

"It's my absolute honour I have your trust, Your Serene Highness." I hid my wicked grin behind a graceful smile, the one that had deceived everyone I met. Everyone besides Jade. Well, whatever her name was.

From the corners of my eyes, I caught Leah and two guards approaching the gazebo. Perfect timing on her part. Impressive for her first task. I nudged subtly at them and dipped into a little bow. "I'll take my leave now, Your Serene Highness."

"Thank you for your time, Your Royal Highness Zafira."

I curtsied again, just as Leah and two guards climbed the gazebo and waited patiently at the stairs. "Your Royal Highness, Zafira. At your service."

Instead of having them drag the prince away for a grave punishment, I'd have them escort me back to the palace. I needed him alive and well, stewing in his own frustrations and fears. When I got Jade assassinated, I wanted him to be the first suspect. I wanted gossip, rumours, whispers about his deranged state.

Yes, he'd be a perfect fall guy. And if this started a war, perfect. Maybe I'd get rid of Oumar in one go to when Father realised how useless he was at ruling. What a beautiful opportunity. I loved when the heavens smiled at me with their blessing.

"Leah."

"Yes, Your Royal Highness Zafira?"

"Just 'Your Royal Highness' will do. And send a guard to find princess Jade and have her escorted to my quarters."

"At once, Your Royal Highness." She directed my instructions to the guard, even if he heard me perfectly fine. But if I could avoid it, I didn't like talking directly to the servants. I had a handmaiden for that.

With the sun burning into my back, I happily returned to the shadow of the palace. Leah called all the servants together and they scrambled to me with a refreshing beverage and a nice cold basin for my feet. Orange blossoms bummed against my ankles as I soaked in the cool scented water. Exactly what I needed. Perfect.

Refreshed from my meeting with Franz, I moved up to my private quarters. I still needed to figure out how to dispose of Jade, but I knew I'd recognise the opportunity when it presented itself.

"Azim." I nodded, ignoring Jalal like always. My oldest guard bowed respectfully as he swung the doors open for me. Leah bounced inside my chambers, clearly excited to be here. But I had no need for her, not with the beautiful blonde waiting against the wall.

"Leah, leave us."

For the first time, the young woman hesitated to follow my command. She lingered at the door, seemingly unsure of what to do. "But Your Royal Highness..."

"I don't want to hear any protest. Leave!"

As if struck with lightning, she scurried away and left me alone with Jade. Just how I liked it.

"*Princess*," I said, not veiling my irony well.

"Your Royal Highness."

With my nose in the air, I walked past her into the bedroom. The door shrieked in its hinges as I left it cracked open. Soft hands found my waist as she didn't even wait a moment to join me and I felt myself lean into her touch. What was wrong with me? Why was I enjoying her presence, even though I loathed her?

"You've sent for me, Princess?" Her voice was soft and warm against my air, like the gentle autumn breeze.

"I wanted to see you," I admitted before I could stop myself. Fuck. That wasn't what I meant to say, not even close.

"Missed me?" she flirted, the orchids dancing around me again. She felt like receiving a hug from a beautiful bouquet and it sent shivers down my spine.

"No chance in hell," I retorted, my eloquent words falling out of my head.

"I think that's a yes," she teased, curling her hand around my waist and spinning me around. Her soft breath clashed against my skin as I faced her and her deep green eyes. Beautiful. She was far too beautiful for her own good.

"Shut up," I snapped back, hating how out of control she was making me feel again. I didn't summon her so she could turn me into a helpless puppy again.

A challenging smile curled her lips up. "Make me."

Without wasting another second, I crashed my lips on hers. Orchids against almonds, tender with rough, hate with passion. Our heels clacked on the stone floor as I guided her to the bed and pushed her down. This time, she'd be on the receiving end. I wouldn't allow anything else.

I tore her dress open with no regard for whether she was ready or not. She didn't take the time to check if I was okay last time and I would give her exactly what she dealt out. With a passion, a heat I didn't know I had in me, I wrestled for dominance. Body against body, hands tangled with hair, legs grinding between thighs. She was all over me and it set me on fire. My heart pounded with excitement as I felt her weaken under me and eventually give up. This time, I was in charge.

Through the struggle, her dress had fallen open and exposed her beautiful breasts. Greedily, I immediately went for the perked up pink bud and sucked it between my lips. Jade gasped under me, her hands traveling up my thighs. I flicked my tongue across, eliciting another sigh from her and somehow, it made me feel smug. Very smug. I was enjoying this far more than expected and I wasn't sure if it even had anything to do with the dominance. Maybe there was something else going on, something else I didn't really understand.

I grazed my teeth over the sensitive bud and the blonde dug her nails into my thigh. With a growl, I bit harder, rewarding her for her response. The soft sting of her nails was pleasant in a twisted way and I wasn't opposed to a little pain. Not if I was in control of it. Although I couldn't deny being bent over my own bed was terribly exciting. But I'd never let her do that to me again. My pride wouldn't allow it.

Instead, I breathed in the orchids and traveled across her smooth stomach. She let out a little moan as I shoved her legs open and it sent a tingle straight to my core. Everything about her, everything about this was far too exciting. I couldn't stop. I didn't want to stop.

Chapter 20. Red

"TAKE OFF YOUR DRESS," Jade murmured, her eyes clouded with lust.

"I am, but not because you're telling me to." I really wanted to take off my clothes so I could feel her skin against mine, but I couldn't have her believing she was in charge.

"I don't care, as long as you take it off."

My dress coiled in a heap somewhere on the floor and I finally felt all of Jade's smoothness against me. Her long legs, her strong arms, her heaving chest. The warmth of her breath, the tremble of her hips, the wetness between her thighs. I slid my fingers along her folds, teasing her mercilessly until her own hand traveled down. I caught it and pinned it above her head.

"No touching," I scolded playfully, kissing her quickly while I had my lips up there. I'd soon be using them for something else, something that would have her melting against me.

"But you're so nice to touch", Jade purred.

"Too bad." I gave her another quick peck, finally recognising the taste of nectarines. With the sweet taste dancing on my tongue, I trailed butterfly kisses down her stomach, just like last time. The blonde sucked in her breath as I approached the soft mound between her thighs. A murmur fell from her lips as she spread her legs even wider and exposed herself to me. With her arousal visible, it was hard to deny myself the pleasure.

Without waiting, I slipped a finger inside of her and earned myself a low rumble from deep within her chest. With her head tipped back into the pillow and her legs spread open, she was a sight to behold. The soft moans, the insistent touches, the willingness... She was poetry under my fingers.

Like the other day, I searched for the hidden bundle of nerves and grinned as her body spasmed up. It only took a little flick to set her body on fire and the pleasure emitting from her had me twitching in anticipation. Even if I didn't like admitting it, I was craving her touch. I wanted her fingers inside of me, to feel that same pleasure as last time, but I couldn't. Instead, I slipped one of her legs between mine and trapped it against me. The tingling was turning into neediness and with every moan, every sigh, it became harder to control it. With every buck of her hips, her upper thigh ground sexily against my trembling core. I knew I was leaving a wet patch, but I didn't care. It felt too good, too slippery, too forbidden. I wasn't about to stop or be stopped, not this time.

"Turn around," I whispered, curling my finger inside her.

"What?" The haze in her eyes was undeniably from clouds of lust.

"Turn around," I repeated myself, a little firmer. I tugged on her long legs, urging her to flip. Grumpily, the blonde turned on her soft stomach and gave me a good view off her ass. With a devious grin, I stroked the small of her back until I reached the firm cheeks and slapped them.

"Hey!" Jade shouted, but her voice betrayed just how sexy she found it.

"What?" I mimicked, spanking her again. The sound slashed through the room and bounced against the walls. I loved it.

"Stop it," she moaned, but from all the squirming it didn't actually seem like she wanted me to stop. Good. I wasn't actually planning to.

My palm connected to the soft cheek again, drawing redness to the surface. With my nails edging lines in her back and my hand splashing colour on her skin, I had the blonde moaning under me. Her desperate wiggle as I ignored the good parts was quite funny and I fully intended on making her squirm and beg under me.

"Stop spanking my ass," Jade groaned, pushing herself up. The muscles on her back rippled under her smooth skin in a mesmerising motion and I found myself pushing her back down.

"Stay." Ignoring the scent of orchids and the whimpers falling from her lips, I pinned her down and brought my hand down again.

"Stop it! Slap me one more time. I dare you."

"Or what?" I asked, mischief bubbling up in my stomach.

"You'll find out."

"That sounds like a challenge." With a grin and excitement coursing through me, I connected my palm with her ass again. The blonde snapped up, her eyes glinting with anger and lust.

"You asked for it," she growled, shoving me off her back. With legs entangled and sheets constricting our bodies, she wrestled me down again. She was strong, maybe even stronger than I was. But I wouldn't let her get the best of me. Not this time.

The sting of nails scraping down my back had red flashing in front of my eyes and I bit down on her arm. She roared angrily, but I didn't care. I just took advantage of the moment and kicked her back off of me. If she thought I'd let her get the best of me, she was so wrong.

"Bitch." Jade cursed, spitting at me.

"Cunt," I countered, aiming for her ass one more time. The slap echoed through the room and enraged the blonde even more. Like a raging bull, she threw me off of the bed, sheets and all. I thudded to the stone floor, my shoulder taking the worst of the pain. It took a moment to gather my thoughts again, but too late. She was looming over me with a grin so dark, so twisted, it set fire to my heart. She was radiant like a thousand suns, her black soul rotten through and through. The worst part of all was that I only felt a deep kinship with this devil. When the end of the world came upon us, I'd meet her again in Hell and we'd dance to a tune only we knew.

She chuckled throatily, kneeling down to press my face into the floor as she spanked me until it felt raw and too sensitive. With every slap, the blonde laughed as she humiliated me and to my shame, I only felt myself grow more and more excited.

"Just take it, Zafira," she purred in my ear as she plunged her fingers deep inside of me. The immediate surge of pleasure blanked my head for a moment as I let her defile my body. As much as I hated what she did to me, I couldn't deny how wonderfully good it felt. I could hear just how easily she slipped in and out of me, her fingers degradingly sexy.

I was going to make her pay, I really was... But I wanted to enjoy the sensation of being used for just a little longer. The shame of submission only made the rage burn harder in me and when I unleashed all that anger, Jade wouldn't know what hit her.

"Just face it. You're no match for me," she laughed, her lips curling up devilishly as she slipped her fingers between my folds and pinched my sensitive bud.

"Ouch, fuck you!" I screeched, trying to kick her off again. With her thighs clamped tightly around me, she was using my own technic against me. She was just succeeding better. But not for long. With my pride fueling my anger, I bucked and her hold on me loosened. She growled, her nails curling into my back again in a useless attempt to keep me down.

With another burst, I tossed her off of my back and rolled her into a chokehold. Jade shook in my arms as she clawed at anything and everything she could. Like a wild cat, she flailed and mewled against the grip I had over her. That would teach her.

I held her down with my own bodyweight and used one hand to slip it between the softness of her thighs. The blonde screamed murder, but her excitement betrayed her real feelings. Without any trouble, I slipped my fingers deep inside of her and shut her up in one go. The urgent protests turned into desperate moans, unable to hold back the primal desires ruling her body. I ground myself down on her, using her for my own pleasure as I hunted for her sensitive bud. She bucked in ecstasy as I drew persistent circles on her, her whole frame trembling as her body begged me not to stop.

"Just let it happen," I mocked her, slapping the inside of her thighs degradingly. If she thought she could jerk me around, she picked the wrong opponent.

"Fuck you," she spat back, bucking against me to throw me off.

"Do that again," I teased, her protest providing me with just the right kind of friction.

"I will not!" she hollered back, and yet, with every tremour or spasm her body coiled up as she ground against me in the most delicious way possible.

"Just submit already, Jade," I laughed, pinching her sensitive bundle cruelly. That would teach her for earlier. If she thought I'd just take her abuse and didn't have any tricks up my own sleeve, she had another thing waiting.

"Never!"

"That's what you're saying now." I dealt her another couple of spanks, the reddening skin turning a shade darker. If she didn't have trouble sitting down tomorrow, I'd be very disappointed in myself.

"You bitch!"

"Tell me something I don't know," I bit back, pinching her little bud until she screamed in pain and frustration. A tremble spasmed through her body and I felt her tighten around me. Perfect. From all the struggle, she seemed to be quite exhausted already. Now was my chance.

I kicked her legs open and pinned them down long enough to flick my tongue through her folds. She shuddered against me, her fists falling open as the pleasure obliterated her senses.

"Fuck," she cursed, bucking against me needily. "Don't you dare stop."

Chapter 21. Stop

"WHY WOULD I DO THAT?" I chuckled, my words vibrating against her. The moans I drew from her lips were like the sweetest melody to my ears. With every shake, every pant, every demanding tug on my hair, I felt her growing closer. If I wanted to be a real bitch, I'd play the same game as the last time, but I didn't need her to beg. Her moans were already doing that for her.

"Don't stop," she demanded, but her voice was barely above a whisper. The scent of orchids mingled with the taste of nectarines on my tongue as I licked her folds. With every flick, she twitched involuntarily against me, her hips bucking up as if she was presenting herself to me. With my fingers pushing deep inside of her and her pink bud trembling against me, she wasn't far off being tipped over the edge.

"Should I stop?" I teased, not able to resist my cruel streak. Jade tightened her hand in my hair and shoved my face down.

"No, don't stop," she mewled, pushing herself onto my mouth. With renewed enthusiasm, I applied as much pressure as possible on the sensitive bundle. Jade was someone who always had something to say, but right now, she was speechless. No words made it out of her mouth as she quivered against my tongue, her breathing accelerating with every spasm.

She was close, so close. If I stopped now, I'd ruin her day and that knowledge, that power set fire to my own core. The beauty jerked and bucked against the constant pressure, her moans desperate, her whimpers needy, her pleasure undeniable. Just a little more, a little harder, a little rougher. I shoved my fingers as deep inside of her as I could and bit down on her bud.

"Fuck!" The ecstasy washed over her, wiping all rational thoughts from her brain and turning the powerful woman into a mewling ball of moans. Her eyes rolled into the back of her head as she violently thrashed against me. With a grin, I bit again, turning the pleasure into pain and intensifying the waves rolling over her.

An undecipherable word fell from her lips as she pushed her legs closed, the universal signal that she was done. But I wouldn't let her, no, we were done when I decided we were. I moved with her body's spasms, curling my fingers up against her sensitive spot to prolong the uncontrolled moans and whimpers.

"Stop, stop, I'm done," Jade panted, her hands aimlessly waving at my head to push me away but I ignored her protest. I pinched her again, without any intention of causing her pleasure. No, this was her punishment for using me, for making me beg, for daring to play my game.

"Fuck, stop!"

"I'll stop when I'm done," I laughed, keeping my thumb steadily on her little bud. The blonde thrashed uncontrollably on the floor, rolling and squirming away from my touch to no avail. That served her damn right.

She clenched so tightly onto my fingers, I felt it strain my shoulder but that was by no means a sign to give up. With every little flick, she twitched and shuddered helplessly, involuntarily. The strong and powerful woman was reduced to a whimpering mess just from the mere touch of my fingers and tongue.

"Please, stop." Her desperation fluttered my stomach to life and I wanted more of it. Instead of letting her rest, I stimulated her little bundle of nerves again and earned myself another plea. "I'm done, stop. Please, stop."

Robbed from her strength, she flailed pathetically on the floor as she tried to squirm away from me. I held her down with just one hand and rubbed more circles on her sensitive bud. Every flick shot a violent spasm through her body and had her moaning into the sheets she was clinging to. She was spent, utterly and entirely drawn out.

I dried my hands on the sheets and wiped my mouth. "Now we're done."

"Fuck you!"

I slapped her ass as I got up and chuckled to myself. "I don't think you have the energy for that."

She attempted to kick my legs from underneath me, but there was no force left in her muscles. "You're a real bitch."

"Makes two of us," I shrugged, cladding my naked body in a dressing gown and throwing one on top of the curled up woman on the floor. "Dress yourself," I commanded. I wrapped the soft satin around me, the cool fabric a nice change to Jade's heated body.

"I should just push you out of the window," she threatened.

"Maybe stop shaking first," I suggested, not at all impressed. She was only just returning to her snappy self and it would take a little longer before she regained her full strength.

"Ha. Ha." She hid the scratches on her body with the robe and slapped my leg. "Make room."

"Such ladylike manners," I mocked, wondering how many hints I could make until she started to suspect something. Playing in on her paranoia would be fun. Maybe I could even make her believe she was losing it. And then right as everything dawned on her, as she realised I played her... I'd kill her. She'd die with the permanent look on her face of someone that got bested in life and I'd make damn sure that was her last thought before the light went out.

"I think we can both agree that the need for royal stiffness went out of the window when you shackled me to your bed," she smiled, her fingers walking over my thigh.

"That was a lovely night," I mused, glad I got to make up for the interruption.

"Such a lovely night," Jade replied sarcastically. She inspected some of the bruises on her arm and sighed. "No short sleeves tomorrow then."

"I'm wearing a scarf tomorrow." Without even looking, I knew she left her own marks scattered across my skin.

"Talking about tomorrow, I guess I'll see you at the banquet." Jade pushed a lock of hair behind her ear and smiled. "I'll get to spend some time with your beloved brother."

"Yes, how wonderful," I muttered, a strange twang shooting through my stomach at the thought of her sucking up to my brother. Oumar was a distasteful man and I knew he'd be enamored by the beautiful Jade. There was no chance in hell he wouldn't want to marry her, but I couldn't let that happen. Exposing or disposing of Jade while she was married to my brother wouldn't actually help me in my conquest. He'd just remarry and I'd be back where I started.

No, I couldn't allow that. I'd have to get rid of her before she tricked my brother into marrying him, no matter what Franz said. I didn't care about him or his sister and if they wanted to declare war, that was their problem. I only had eyes for Jade. Now I knew what her true nature was like, it seemed unlikely that I'd manage to make her do my bidding. Jade wasn't easily manipulated, but that made it such a challenge.

"I can't wait to meet your brother tomorrow."

"Good luck with that." I clicked my tongue and ran a hand through my silky hair. I could feed her false information so she'd embarrass herself terribly. She'd get rejected and Father would send her away after the failed matchmaking. But then again... No Jade anymore...

"Can I give you some advice?"

"Go ahead." She didn't hide her suspicious look very well, but I didn't care. "He hates the taste of cinnamon, so don't touch anything cinnamony. You're lucky with your looks, he has a profound weakness for women with dimples in their cheeks. He loves to make bad jokes, so be prepared for a lot of fake laughing. He hates dogs, absolutely can't stand them, so don't bring them up. And never, ever, take the last grape."

Jade pulled up an eyebrow as she studied my face. "And how do I know you're telling the truth?"

I shrugged. "Why wouldn't I?"

"Maybe you're feeding me the wrong answers so I'll make a fool out of myself."

"Maybe." I caught her gaze and admired the dark glint in them. "Or maybe I'm helping you."

She laughed harshly, her hair dancing around her face in the breeze passing through. "And what reason could you possibly have for helping me?"

"Maybe I just want my brother to find a good wife." I paused, waiting for dramatic effect. "Or maybe I like having you around," I admitted softly, almost believing my own lie. Maybe it was truer than I wanted to admit.

"Maybe I like *being* around you," Jade smiled, her fingers brushing softly over my lips. The wind caught in my hair and the blonde pushed some disheveled locks behind my ear. "You're beautiful."

A weird sensation bubbled up in my stomach, a warmth I didn't really understand. There was something odd, something strange in the way she was looking at me and I didn't like not understanding it. I averted my gaze and ignored her compliment. She was doing weird things to me, turning my head upside down. I couldn't let her.

"When he grabs your ass, and I can assure you he will... Let him," I added, bringing her attention back to the topic at hand.

Jade's face turned sour and her hand dropped back into her lap. "Is that why you slapped me raw?"

I grimaced. "That'll sting nicely tomorrow. Call it a reminder of tonight."

"I should've guessed." She slipped off the window sill and gently touched my cheek. "With that in mind, I should return to my chambers. It's late and I want to give my ass a good rest."

"Thank you for a lovely evening," I said, my voice not as sarcastic as I'd wanted it to be. The moonlight danced on her curves as her dressing gown slipped off her shoulders and i couldn't but admire her. With every dip and curve highlighted, it was hard not to be in awe of the beauty in front of me.

"It was a pleasure." Jade slipped into her dress, sighing at the ripped open side. "Zip me up?"

The stone floor was cold under my feet as I tip-toed over to the blonde. The metal shrieked in protest, the harsh noise breaking the silence of the night. As I concealed the bruises and scratches, I felt compelled to kiss her. Without really knowing why, I pressed a butterfly peck down on her naked shoulder before the dress hid her from me.

"There, all zipped up."

"Thank you." She dipped her head, the darkness never really leaving her eyes. "Zafira."

I rested against the wall, a smirk playing on my lips. "Jade."

"I'll see you tomorrow, sleep well." Without waiting for my reply, she swayed to the door and disappeared into the darkness. I tossed the tangled up sheets back on the bed and fell down on the mattress, replaying the events in my head. The moans and whimpers of Jade echoed in my head as images of her naked body flashed through my mind. But they didn't silence that one odd thought in the back of all my thoughts. I replayed the evening over and over, hoping to obliterate the strange wish lingering in my chest.

That I'd wanted her to stay.

Chapter 22. Oumar

"MORE REFRESHMENTS, Your Royal Highness Zafira?" One of the servants asked, bowing deeply as he presented me with more water. I waved my fan at Leah and she declined in my stead. I did hate all the dreadful, dreadful banquets and ceremonies. I wasn't really allowed to speak to anyone, eat much, or breathe too loudly. The decorations had wilder adventures than I did.

The servants kept rotating plates arrayed with colourful fruits and vegetables in front of my nose, but I wasn't actually allowed to eat from them. All I got was herby spreads that were good for my waistline and digestion. Boring. But it was Father's idea of keeping me pure and beautiful, like a flower. If only he knew what I'd been up to for the past years. He wouldn't have to wait for the cancer to get to him, it would kill him instantly.

I nibbled on some bread, enjoying the herby flavours mingling on my palate. The spreads were beautifully garnished with edible flowers that reminded me of Jade. At least the cooks made an effort today.

I studied the beautiful blonde at the other end of the hall. It was highly improper for her to be chatting with Oumar, but he invited her up and we all knew that men got their way even if it wasn't technically allowed. He whispered something in her ear and even from here, I heard her crystal laugh. She was playing the perfect part. Engaging, innocent, foreign.

To her credit, I'd never have guessed she wasn't a true royal. She definitely had that inherent grace and knack for lying down.

"Leah."

"Yes, Your Royal Highness?"

"Go serve His Royal Highness Oumar his favourite orange tea. And have a listen to what the two of them are discussing." Sneaky, but I couldn't stand not knowing what was going on.

"At once, Your Royal Highness."

Oumar's laugh boomed across the hall and from Jade's smug grin, I knew it was because of her. Of course it was because of her. How could he not be charmed by this amazing, mysterious, and beautiful woman?

Hah, at least I already bedded her. Take that, Brother.

I glared at the two of them, glad I could hide behind my fan. It made it very easy to spy without being seen or have the jealousy revealed.

No, that wasn't right. I didn't do jealousy because that actually meant liking something, or someone. And I didn't like Jade, not in that way. I was possessive. She was my toy and he was playing with her.

My plans to kill my brother turned a shade crueler and I wondered if I should just poison him right now. If I blamed the foreigners for it, I might get away with it. And at least I didn't have to see his grubby hands on her.

"Your Royal Highness?"

"What is it?" I turned to Leah, surprised that I actually snapped. What was happening? Was my mask faltering? Why did this Oumar-Jade thing get so on my nerves?

"I served His Royal Highness Oumar and had a listen to the conversation. Your Royal Highness"

"Excellent. What are they discussing? Was it proper?"

"Yes, Your Royal Highness. Just discussing the weather."

"I see. You're dismissed."

She bowed, obstructing my view of Jade. Annoyed, I waved her away and kept glaring in their general direction. I just wanted this stupid banquet to be over so I could have Jade tied in my room again. Maybe this time, I'd keep her shackled so she couldn't escape and make googly eyes at my brother.

I turned to the throne and put on my best smile. "May I be excused? I would like to catch some fresh air."

Mother scoffed, the bitterness drawing ugly lines in her face. She always envied my beauty and youth and with every passing day, she became worse at hiding her disdain for me. Why Father broke tradition and decided to only have one wife instead of a harem like his predecessors was a mystery to me. Especially since his one wife was Mother, a sour and envious old woman.

"Father?" I ignored Mother's glare and directed my request to him. I really wanted some fresh air instead of having to spend another second looking at the ridiculous show Jade was putting up.

"Be excused, my child." He dismissed me with a smile, the crow feet showing along his eyes. He was too exhausted to care and I almost pitied him for falling ill. But then, I'd pitied him his whole life. Once, he probably commanded a lot of respect, but the man sitting on this throne was a shadow of himself. A puppet that didn't deserve to be ruling. Especially not if he had a perfectly good successor sitting at his feet.

My servants scrambled as I rose from my seat and strode towards the gardens. From the corners of my eyes, I caught Jade looking at me and a strange tingling filled my stomach. I liked it. No, I deserved it. She should be looking at me instead of hanging at Oumar's lips.

I should just kill him and get it over with. The only problem was how, and I hadn't yet figured that out yet.

My footsteps echoed in the corridor on my way to the gardens. The sun was calling my name and I looked forward to be out of the constricting walls.

"Your Royal Highness. You sent for me?"

I turned on my heels, surprised to find Halim waiting for me. I had completely forgotten about him. I'd been too preoccupied with Jade.

Bitterness welled up in me as I saw her laughing at Oumar's stupid jokes. He didn't deserve her company.

"I sent for you days ago," I smiled politely, glaring at my group of handmaidens. Whoever I sent that day, had done an awful job if he only showed up days later.

"I didn't get the message, Your Royal Highness."

I scanned my servants, my eyes falling on a familiar face. "You. Did you send for him when I commanded you?"

The woman fell to her knees and sobbed. "I did, Your Royal Highness. I swear, I left a message for him at the barracks."

"I see. Leah, give us a moment." Whatever the reason was, he hadn't shown up when I had needed him and now he was casually addressing me in public. "What do you want?"

Halim took a step forward, his lewd smile not even hidden very well. "It's been a while since we explored the dungeons, Your Royal Highness. I'm experiencing some... Withdrawal."

"I've been very busy, Halim." I glared at him, appalled by his forwardness.

"I understand that, but I have... certain needs. And if I can't relieve this itch, bad things could happen. I might say things you'd rather not want anyone hearing," he grinned, his face lit up like a child. Did he really think he could blackmail me? At what point did this poor bastard think I was providing him a service instead of the other way around?

"Are you threatening me?" I demanded, disgusted by the glee in his eyes.

"Threatening? Oh no, of course not, Your Royal Highness. This is just a mere request from your humble servant."

"I see. Thank you for bringing this to my attention, I'll see to it immediately. Meet me at the Summer Resort tonight."

"The Summer Resort?"

"Yes, where Princess Jade is staying."

"Princess Jade?"

"Exactly."

His whole face lit up in delight. He was clearly lusting over her already. "Perfect. I'll be there." He grinned pervertedly, his eyes filled with desire. "Your Royal Highness."

He turned on his heels and strode away, his steps filled with arrogance. Appalling. But I would make sure to deal with him tonight and punish him properly.

The grass brushed past my ankles and the rays of sun danced along my skin. I snapped at the maids to get me some shade to accompany me to the gazebo.

"Stay." I barked, leaving the servants at the foot of the stairs. I wanted some solitude and I had no need for the annoying chattering of the women around me.

A breeze danced around me and carried the scent of wildflowers along. The floral notes lifted some of the moodiness and filled my lungs with clean air. The scent of orchids mingled with the other flowers and I sensed her presence before I heard her.

"Your Royal Highness, Princess Jade is requesting to join you," Leah called up from the bottom of the gazebo.

I nodded. "Let her up."

"Your Royal Highness," she smiled, her scent growing stronger until she was standing right behind me.

"Princess."

"I heard you excused yourself from the banquet. Are you not feeling well?"

"Fresh air serves me well."

"Liar."

I raised my eyebrow. "Excuse me?" What was going on today? Why was everyone so blunt? Did they forget who I was?

"I saw you looking at me with that disapproving stare."

"I don't know what you're talking about," I denied, fanning myself gently in an attempt to hide my lies.

"You know exactly what I'm talking about." Briefly, she touched my waist so softly, it could've been mistaken for a flutter of wind. "Are you jealous, Zafira?"

"Jealous? Hah, I don't know what that means."

She snickered softly, her blonde hair dancing in the warm breeze. "It makes you feel like there's a brick on your stomach, like your lungs are clenched shut, as if someone is squeezing your heart." She turned towards me, her eyes boring into my rotten soul. "Do you know what it's like to feel, Your Royal Highness?"

"Of course, I feel," I lied.

"No, not that kind of feel." Jade let out a throaty chuckle, her hand dancing from my waist to my hand. She paused a moment before placing her palm against my chest. "This kind."

"No," I admitted, mesmerized by her voice. Even if I didn't feel, not like normal people, I still experienced something when I was around her. Something I didn't have around anyone else.

Jade flashed me a brief smile, her mask slipping for a moment. "Me either. But we got really good at pretending, didn't we?"

"We sure did," I chuckled. "Do you ever get tired of it?"

"Of what?"

"Of having to live this... this lie. Having to hide who we *really* are."

"Sometimes... But then I remember how fun it is to mess with people."

"People really are stupid." I hummed. "That reminds me, I've sent you a present. He will arrive tonight at the resort."

"He?" An excited flicker danced through her eyes.

"That's what I said."

"Someone to play with?" Jade asked, licking her lips.

"Yes, but save me some of the fun."

The blonde chuckled softly. "Will do."

"I bet you it's more exciting than talking to my *sweet, beloved brother*," I mocked quietly, pulling a face at the thought of Oumar. I really, really hated him.

"You sure you're not jealous?" Jade clicked her tongue and grinned.

"I don't do jealous," I snapped. Instantly, I turned on my heels and hid behind my fan. "Princess."

"Your Royal Highness."

With a little curtesy, I left the blonde in the gazebo. My servants ran around me to provide me with the necessary shade, but I no longer cared. Jade wasn't sucking up to my brother and damn it, I was *not* jealous.

Chapter 23. Bloodhound

THE EVENING BREEZE tickled my skin as I rushed through the shadows of the palace walls to the Summer Resort. The light in the highest tower had flicked on not long ago and I took it as a sign that Hamil presented himself to Jade.

The door to the secret entrance shrieked softly, but there wasn't anyone around to hear it anyway. The stairs curled up to the balcony and I found Jade leaning against one of the pillars.

"You're late," she mused, brushing a strand behind her ear. But the wind had different thoughts and a passing gust had her blonde hair tangling in front of her face.

"Missed me?" I smiled, cupping her face and wiping my thumb across her cheek.

"Terribly. I waited for you to unwrap my present."

"You shouldn't have." I stole a quick kiss from her lips and followed her into the room. Apart from a couple of candles, there wasn't a single sign we used it for our twisted games before. And the man strapped to the table.

"Hello, Halim." I nodded at him, greeted with a muffled scream. He thrashed against the ropes, his whole face painted with angry hard lines. I pulled the cloth out of his mouth and was immediately greeted with his complaints.

"What is the meaning of this?" he shouted, glaring angrily at Jade. The blonde shrugged and coiled some of the spare rope around her hand. He turned back to me, foam bubbling up from his mouth. He clearly wasn't used to being the one tied down instead of doing it. "I thought you set it up for me!"

"I did."

"Not what I meant, Princess! I told you I have urges that need to be satisfied."

"And what makes you think you won't get what you want?"

Jade studied me, her dark eyes filled with an curious glint. "Why did he come here, Zafira?"

I shrugged. "To fuck you."

"Aha, I see." She pushed herself away from the wall and circled the table. Her slender fingers traced playfully over Halim's chest and she chuckled. "Did you want him to succeed?"

"You'll never know." I curled my arm around her waist and caught her in a kiss. "Isn't that exciting."

"Very." She nipped at my bottom lip and entwined her tongue with mine. The softness of her touch and the urgency of her kiss danced through my body in a whirlwind of shivers. Her touch, her scent, her taste, everything about her was intoxicating, irresistible, addictive and I couldn't get enough of her.

"Hot." Halim chuckled on the table and I recognised the perverted look in his eyes. He still thought he was getting some. Oh, the fool.

"You think so?" She took a step back and trailed her fingers along his leg. The innocent smile along her lips could've fooled anyone, but me. I knew what devilish thoughts she hid behind it.

"Hell yes."

She let out one of her signature throaty chuckles and brushed her hand through his hair. He wetted his lips, his eyes beaming with excitement. "I could use some help downstairs."

How crude. He truly deserved to be punished for his insubordination and now the way he spoke to Jade. He didn't know she wasn't a real princess and yet he took such liberties? How distasteful.

"Talkative, isn't he?" Jade turned to me, her voice betraying the playfulness of her nature. It took me a moment to figure out what she meant, but then I caught on. I balled the dirty cloth behind my back and swayed closer to the table.

"Very talkative," I agreed, winking at the blonde.

"Right, this was very funny and all, but now I'm ready to be serviced." He sounded confident, but the slight elevation of his voice completely undermined his arrogance. He wasn't as in control as he liked to be and he was finally realising it.

"Should I?" I tilted my head and held the cloth out in front of me.

"It would be a pleasure," Jade grinned.

"Wait! You're not going to put that back in, right?" Halim strained against the ropes. "Right?" His voice cracked, the first signs of panic shining through. Perfect.

"Wouldn't I?" I bent over him, using the gag to wipe some of the sweat from his forehead. Halim visibly relaxed and I couldn't believe how stupid he really was. He'd seen me do my false sense of security many times before, and yet he wouldn't recognise it now? How disappointing.

"Haha... Okay, untie me now."

"How cute, he thinks he can give out commands," Jade mused, tapping his nose.

"He can try." I pressed his cheeks together and forced his jaw open. Unceremoniously, I shoved the sweaty cloth into his mouth. "Or not."

The panic finally reached Halim's eyes and he fought against the restraints, harder than any woman before him.

"Think he finally caught on?" I asked Jade, shaking my head in disappointment. "Did he really think I wouldn't punish him for his failures?"

"Such childlike innocence," she tutted, patting his cheek condescendingly. The devious glint in her eyes made it all the more exciting.

"Oh, he isn't very innocent. No, he's a real naughty boy." I poked his leg. "He loves to take women without their permission."

"Oh no," Jade gasped fakely.

"Oh yes. He gets all excited when they're bound and wailing in pain."

The blonde clacked her tongue as she circled Halim. "Dirty, dirty boy."

"And now he disappointed me? Letting poor Farah escape?" I laughed harshly and slapped his cheek. "Did you know some cruel woman turned her into a scarecrow? Yes, you heard that right. Chopped off her head and just shoved a stake in her severed neck."

My bloodhound, my guard dog, my perverted tool turned white as the blood pulled out of his face. With wide eyes, he flicked his gaze from me to Jade and back again. The blonde chuckled and patted his other cheek.

"Don't look at me, I'm the cruel woman she's speaking of. A bit harsh, don't you think, Zafira?"

"Maybe a little. After all, you gave Jamila a nice quick death." I stroked Halim's hair, the vindictive streak in me flaring up. "But that won't be the case for dear Halim here."

Halim thrashed against his constraints, the panic crystal clear against his gag. The muffled sounds wouldn't leave this room, no matter how loud he screamed.

"No, he deserves a real punishment," Jade agreed, the excitement lighting up her face and red blushes colouring her cheeks. Beautiful. There was nothing more beautiful than a woman enjoying herself and there was no doubt she was.

I clicked Halim's belt open and curled my fingers around his waistband. With one quick tug, I exposed his prized jewel to the cold air.

"Pathetic." Jade rolled her eyes and bent over Halim. "What a tiny little prick."

He growled loudly, but his threat lost all power with him tied to the table with his pants down his ankles. He truly was pathetic. A bark without bite.

"He loves shoving himself in other women... I think it's time we punished him accordingly."

"Oh, it'll be a pleasure." The blonde caught my eyes and blew a kiss my way. A flutter danced through my chest and I couldn't remember when I had this much fun. All the manipulating and sorrow I sowed wasn't anything compared to the joy of having someone just as twisted by my side to make everything worse.

Maybe keeping Jade wasn't the worst idea I ever had. She still needed to be punished properly, but maybe death wasn't it. It was quite permanent and quick, not at all suited for what I had in mind.

No, I could keep her around for a bit longer, just until I figured out the right way to deal with her. It was in the interest of retribution, not because I'd grown quite fond of her. I didn't do that, that involved me actually caring about someone.

And I didn't care about Jade. Not at all.

I stole a glimpse of the blonde as she slapped Halim's flaccid member with a piece of wood. She was gorgeous, smart, wicked, and made from the same cloth as I was. But no, I didn't care about her at all. She was another tool, just like everyone else.

"How do you want to punish him for his poor servitude?" The glee shone through in Jade's silky voice and it only added to my own excitement. I was going to enjoy this moment. It was the first time Jade and I would be unleashing all our twisted thoughts on the same person, together.

Jamila and Farah didn't count, that was just her putting on a show for me. But this time, we'd be accomplishing utter devastation between the two of us. Like a twisted date.

I reached back and pulled some hair clips from my elaborate bun. My dark hair cascaded down my shoulders and elicited a smirk from the beauty in front of me. I curled the strands up in a quick ponytail and held out the sharp clips so Halim could see them.

"I have these," I sang, passing them to the blonde. The muffled screams of our victim intensified with the metal click as she popped them open.

"How cruel," Jade noted, her voice shimmering with respect. "Impressive."

"Ladies first," I offered, earning a smile from the blonde.

"With pleasure." The lower she brought the hairclip, the harder Halim fought against his constraints. The ropes drew red lines into the skin, but this pain was nothing compared to what was coming. His panicked noises and muffled screams encouraged Jade to scrape the metal pin over the wrinkled skin. He sucked in his breath, his cries and whimpers more and more pathetic with every moment. "Where should I put it?"

"Through the side? Maybe put it in the tip"

"I like that." The sharp pin of the hair clip pushed the skin back and slid surprisingly easy into the tip. Halim bucked up, veins popping up along his forehead and the pain was sprawled across his face. With his fists balled and the ropes digging hard into his wrists and ankles, the bloodhound morphed into a whimpering baby.

His pathetic sniffles and cries only edged on the blonde and a devious grin broke through on her face. "All the way through this time?" The metal pin punctured the first layer of skin and Halim thrashed so hard against the ropes I feared they'd break. He screamed into the gag, spittle drooping down his jaw. I pulled the cloth from his mouth, interested in what he had to say.

"You bitches!" he cursed. The big vein along his forehead threatened to explode at any moment as he fought against his predicament. No luck. He was well and truly tied down and at Jade and I's mercy. And she didn't know the meaning of that word either.

"That's not very nice to say," Jade tutted, jabbing the pin all the way through his member. The exasperated cries and howls from Halim were music to my ears. He truly deserved the pain after all the disappointment he caused. I just hoped he was feeling the full extent of my wrath.

From the desperate look on his face, he probably was.

"Do his balls," I egged Jade on.

"No, no, no, not my balls!" His curses turned into pleas as Jade pierced the wrinkled skin and stabbed the sharp pin straight through his sack. There wasn't a word to describe the immense pain echoing in his screams or the hurt edged into his features.

"Gag him, he's too loud."

She was right. If he kept it up, someone might actually hear him and get suspicious. I shoved the rag back in his mouth and silenced most of his cries. With every twist of the hairpin, Halim's eyes rolled further into the back of his skull and I feared he was going to pass out soon.

"He talks a lot, but he's a bit of a wuss, isn't he?" The disappointment shone through in her voice and I shrugged.

"He was always pathetic," I voiced, not sure why she was surprised at how quickly guys submitted.

"Can't even take a little hairpin to the balls."

"If it wouldn't spill so much blood, I'd just cut them off."

Halim cried into his gag, sniveling and bleating worse than any of his victims. I was sure any of the women he raped would love the sight of me stripping him from his power, his manhood. I really wished I could just snip the whole thing off, but that would rouse too much suspicion.

"Can I?" I asked, reaching out to the piece of wood Jade was using earlier.

"With pleasure," she smiled, handing me the paddle. I twirled it in my hands, admiring the delicate lines running along the wood. Beautiful. Without waiting another second, I slammed it hard into his groin. The wails coming from the heap of misery resembled that of drowning kittens and weren't actually exciting. Just pathetic and weak.

"I think he passed out," Jade noted, poking his leg.

"I believe you are correct." I ground the baton down, wondering if that would wake him back up.

"That was a bit of an anti-climax."

I shrugged. "This is why men aren't fun to torture."

"They truly are pathetic. Not that entertaining as expected."

"My apologies, Princess." I reached out over the unconscious man and kissed her hand. She briefly cupped my cheek and smiled, her eyes lighting up like stars in the sky.

"I enjoyed myself, thank you, Zafira."

I inspected Halim. "Are we done with him?"

"Wack that stick down a couple more times and then I think so."

"Your wish is my command," I winked, earning a soft chuckle. With the back end of the baton, I slammed it into his groin and smashed his family jewels. He'd never be able to fulfil any of his dark desires again, but where he was going, he wouldn't need his member anyway. "Hand me the candle."

Jade's face lit up. "What are you going to do with it?"

"He's seen far too many things," I answered cryptically. I'd have to make sure Halim would never be able to tell anyone about what went on in the dungeons. I peeled his heavy eyelids open and dripped the hot wax onto his eyeballs. With a sizzle, it burned through his irises and left a scorch mark around his eyes. "But now he won't be able to see at all."

"What else?" Jade asked, biting her lip impatiently.

"We don't want him talking, do we?"

"That would certainly complicate things."

"Could I use your knife?" I asked politely, as if we were exchanging handkerchiefs.

"You know where it is," she teased. With a little laugh, I moved towards the blonde and reached inside of her dress. My fingers brushed past her smooth skin until they met the cold steel of her thin dagger. The blade glinted in the candlelight as I held it above the tiny flames. The fire licked at the metal, heating up the knife until it glowed red. Perfect. That would definitely burn and render his throat unusable.

Without having to ask what I was up to, Jade forced his jaw open and exposed the pink inside for me. The blade sizzled as it slashed into his tongue and the back of his throat. With some luck, I'd sever his vocal cords and leave him mute for the rest of his pathetic life. The scent of burned flesh wafted up from the cauterised wounds and I couldn't say it was pleasant. "That should do."

Jade yawned. "Now what? I'm not disposing of another body."

"We untie him and thrash the place. You'll have to pretend he tried to rape you, but I'm sure you won't have any trouble lying about that."

She chuckled and chased the grin away right before my eyes. Her eyes widened, her lips trembled, and a devastated expression made way for her glee. "G-Guards, please help me! This man tried to violate me. My goodness, I can't imagine what would've happened if he, if he... Oh God," she cried, dramatically falling in my arms.

"Perfect."

It only took a couple of minutes to turn the immaculate room into an absolute dump. Curtains torn to shreds, candles spilling wax all over the floor, and an unconscious broken man with bruises and burns scattered along his body.

I kissed Jade gently, enjoying the softness of her lips against mine. I'd have to take my leave now and I didn't want to. I enjoyed her presence, her company, just her. But for this trickery to work, we needed to play the part.

After another kiss, I disappeared back into the night, ready for Jade to awaken the whole palace. Excitement swirled through my veins as I was acutely aware that at any point, she could turn against me. Ready to combat her accusations with my own. This was a dangerous game to play and I loved every moment of it.

The moon travelled through the sky and changed windows before a blood-chilling screech echoed from the Summer Resort. *Play time.*

Chapter 24. Smoke

LIGHTS FLICKED ON, guards marched through the silent halls, and women cried out into the night. The whole palace was in complete chaos for many more hours before the commotion finally died down and everyone went back to their posts or bed.

Jade played her part brilliantly. The big silver tears, the torn dress, the devastated sobs as she clung to the first guard who found her. Her theatrics were performance worthy and I admired her from afar. Despite Halim being the palace master's son, the guards didn't take pity on him. They hung him in the middle of the grounds and he awaited his final punishment in the morning. I couldn't have planned it better.

I waited until the silence fell back over the palace before I snuck back out to the Summer Resort. There were multiple guards waiting at the main entrance, but nobody at the secret passage way. Excellent. I followed the stairs up to the second floor and aimed straight for the master bedroom where my blonde was staying. The breeze played with the curtains and Jade's hair as she awaited my arrival on her bed.

"You took your time," she noted dryly as she stretched herself out on the satin sheets.

"I couldn't risk being seen."

"And yet, here you are."

I brushed my hand over the smooth linen. "Here I am."

Her lips curled up in a smile and she patted the empty spot next to her. "Join me."

If it'd been anyone else, I wouldn't have obeyed. But this didn't sound like a command, more like a request. The bed dipped under me, the moonlight illuminating our two bodies as I laid down next to the beautiful blonde.

"That was an eventful night," Jade remarked, her fingers brushing over my hip.

"It certainly was," I agreed. There hadn't been a moment where the scent of orchids had been stronger than in her bed and the floral notes danced past me with every breeze. There was something beautiful, something magical about the moment, but I didn't know why. Why had Jade this effect on me and how could I make it stop?

Did I even want it to stop?

"I haven't thanked you properly for your present," she smiled, her hand travelling from my waist along my arm. Her fingers walked teasingly along my skin to my lips and I pressed a chaste kiss against the tips.

"I'm right here."

She cupped my cheek and placed the softest kiss on my lips. That same weird flutter awoke in my stomach and rampaged through me with every kiss, every flick, every sigh. There was something in me, something only she woke up and I wanted to explore it. Desperately.

With tender kisses and careful strokes, Jade unzipped my dress and slipped the fabric from my shoulders. I should've protested, but it didn't seem right in the moment. No, the only thing I wanted right now was to feel her lips, her skin, her touch.

Her lips planted soft kisses all along my neck and I didn't know if it was just in my head or not, but it felt different. She felt different. Softer. Warmer. Loving, almost.

With guarded strokes and urgent touches, her hand made its way between my thighs and this time, I willingly opened my legs for her. She rewarded me with a passionate kiss as she slipped her fingers deep inside of me.

The instant bliss dawned on me and for once, I let myself be free to fully enjoy Jade's ministrations. The flicks, the curled fingers, the insistent pressure. The waves rapidly grew inside of me until the last of her strokes pushed me over the edge and they crashed over me. The pleasure dominated my brain for as long or as short as I could make out with the haze raging through my senses.

"Thank you for the present," Jade grinned, quickly pecking my lips. A little embarrassed I gave in so easily, I slipped out of the sheets and draped my dress loosely over my body. I brushed fabric down and prepped myself up on the window sill under the silver shine of the moon.

The blonde wrapped the sheets around her and reached for the nightstand. After a quick rummage, she held up the wrinkled package of smokes and a dinged lighter. Clearly one of her dirty little secrets. "Smoke?"

"I'll have one." There was something peaceful about smoking, especially after some stress relief.

Jade smiled, joining me at the window. The metal clicked as she rolled the wheel of the lighter and the flame sprung up. She held her hand around the tiny flame to protect it from the night breeze and offered it to me first. I took in a deep breath and the red ring curled into the white paper of the fag. The smoke tickled my nose as I took my first drag, the harsh taste of tobacco and tar coating my tongue and filling my lungs. It was a disgusting habit, but a guilty pleasure.

"I wouldn't have pegged you as the smoking type," Jade smiled.

"That goes both ways."

"How did you pick it up?"

I shrugged, inhaling another drag and holding the smoke down for a moment. "One of the inner guards used to smoke quite a lot. He wasn't particularly careful where he left his packages. I'm sure you can guess the rest."

"I can."

"What about you?"

"My nanny smoked a ton. I stole my first one from her and then made my servants get them for me."

"Elegant," I chuckled, bumping my leg against hers. She looked down and her lips curled up in a smile. Her free hand brushed past my thigh in another tender touch. It was hard to believe this was the same person as before

"A girl does what a girl has to do," she shrugged, taking another drag and holding up the bud.

The moon cast a beautiful silver glint on the beauty and I admired her deep green eyes for a moment. She truly was something else. Now that I had more answers, I knew that for sure. But I still had many, many questions.

"Why are you here, Jade?" I looked up into her eyes and dared her to take off her mask.

"In this room? I think you know why," she winked, her grin revealing the smugness in her voice.

"No. In my country."

"I'm here to marry your brother." A glimmer shone in her dark eyes and betrayed the lie.

"I don't believe you. Why are you here?"

The blonde chuckled softly, shaking her head as she wrapped her arms around herself. I reached down for one of my blankets and draped it around her shoulders to combat the cold.

"Do you want to know the truth?" she asked, her voice raising slightly.

"Always."

She let out a short laugh and stared at me, her eyes hard and cold. "I'm here to kill your brother."

I took another drag, pondering over her confession. The last smoke clouded my lungs and I flicked my bud out of the window. The cigarette smouldered for a moment before the dampness of the night got to it and turned to ash. Jade's smoke followed mine and joined it in the grass. The servants would find it and just assume it was from the guards.

"You don't seem shocked." Jade pulled the blanket closer around her and somehow, it made her look vulnerable. Human.

"My brother has many enemies," I stated, shrugging as I studied her. So that was why she was really here?

"Do you make it a habit to sleep with them?" she asked, her fingers wandering aimlessly over my leg.

"No, but I could," I retorted, earning a chuckle from her.

"Maybe you should."

"Depends. Not if you're always bending me over the bed."

"You seemed to like it plenty."

"Fuck you," I grinned, confusing myself with the banter. It was easy to talk to her, especially when we dropped all the pretences. When we weren't fighting over control, it was almost pleasant to be around her.

How odd. I'd never felt that way around anyone before.

"So now you know why I'm here, are you going to spill my little secret?"

"That you're thinking about high treason?"

"If killing the crown prince is considered high treason, than yes."

I chuckled softly. "No, I'm not going to reveal anything."

Jade flashed me a wicked smile. "Why not?"

If she was here to kill Oumar, I had a good reason to keep her around for a little longer. For now, our interest aligned.

I smiled my devilish grin. "Because I'm going to help you."

To be continued...

Read the continuation in Play To Kill

=> https://books2read.com/playtokill

BOOKS IN THE TWISTED *Trilogy*

Book 1: Play To Kiss

Book 2: Play To Kill

Book 3: Play To Keep (TBC)

About Arizona

A CREATOR AT HEART, Ari has always been in love with the idea of turning nothing into something. With her rainbow bat familiar, Sprinkles, she's ready to conquer the book world. Whether it's dragons and vampires or princesses and students, she always knows where to find the romance.

Born in China, raised in Belgium, and currently living in the United Kingdom with her girlfriend, Ari is a citizen of the world and loves discovering new cultures. Luckily, her crazy imagination lets her discover places she's never been to, meet people that don't exist, and talk to readers from all over the world.

Ari is a USA Today Bestselling Author that loves to write all kinds of genres, but her heart belongs to lesbian romance. You can find all her lesfic books under Arizona Tape.

Have a look at my website: https://www.arizonatape.com/books[1]

Looking to connect with me? I'd love that! There are multiple places you can find me, so pick which one you like best.

Website: https://arizonatape.com

Newsletter: https://arizonatape.com/subscribe

Facebook page: https://facebook.com/arizonatype

Facebook Group - Rainbow Central: https://facebook.com/groups/arizonatape

Bookbub: https://bookbub.com/authors/arizona-tape

Twitter: https://twitter.com/arizonatape

Instagram: https://instagram.com/arizonatape

Books by Arizona Tape

MY OWN HUMAN DUOLOGY (completed paranormal dystopian f/f romance)

1. My Own Human: http://books2read.com/myownhuman
2. Your Own Human: http://books2read.com/yourownhuman

My Winter Wolf Trilogy (completed paranormal fantasy f/f romance)

1. Wolf's Whisper: http://books2read.com/wolfswhisper
2. Wolf's Echo: http://books2read.com/wolfsecho
3. Wolf's Howl: http://books2read.com/wolfshowl

- White Wolf, Black Wolf: http://books2read.com/wwbw
- A Squad of Wolves: http://books2read.com/sqad-ofwolves

The Afterlife Academy: Valkyrie (urban fantasy academy f/f)

1. Valkyrie 101: http://books2read.com/valkyrie101
2. Valkyrie 102: http://books2read.com/valkyrie102

Twisted Trilogy (dark contemporary f/f romance)

1. Twisted Games: http://books2read.com/twistedgames
2. Twisted Lives: http://books2read.com/twistedlives

Standalone Contemporary Titles

- The Love Pill: http://books2read.com/lovepill (f/f)
- Not Today: http://books2read.com/nottoday (f/f)
- Four Gamers and Me: http://books2read.com/fourgamersandme (RH with f/f)

Standalone Fantasy

-    Beyond the Northern Lights: http://books2read.com/btnl

Co-Written Books by Arizona Tape

TWIN SOULS TRILOGY, co-written with Laura Greenwood (completed paranormal romance)

1. Soulswap: http://books2read.com/soulswap
2. Soulshift: http://books2read.com/soulshift
3. Soultrade: http://books2read.com/soultrade

- Twins Souls Boxed Set: http://books2read.com/twinsoulstrilogy

Dragon Soul Series, co-written with Laura Greenwood (paranormal romance)

1. Torn Soul: http://books2read.com/tornsoul (also in audio)
2. Bound Soul: http://books2read.com/boundsoul

Renegade Dragons, co-written with Laura Greenwood (completed paranormal romance)

1. Fifth Soul: http://books2read.com/fifthsoul (also in audio)
2. Fifth Round: http://books2read.com/fifthround
3. Fifth Flame: http://books2read.com/fifthflame

Vampire For Hire, co-written with Laura Greenwood (paranormal mystery)

1. Fangs For Nothing: http://books2read.com/ fangsfornothing

Standalone Co-Written Titles

- Partridge in the P.E.A.R, co-written With Skye MacKinnon: http://books2read.com/pear (sci-fi romance)

CPSIA information can be obtained
at www.ICGtesting.com
Printed in the USA
LVHW090407140121
676401LV00015B/1568